Rachel and Harry are planning for the adventure of a lifetime. They are young and in love, and one day they'll be part of the greatest journey ever undertaken. Until then, they're busy with all the preparations, tests and technicalities necessary before they go on board the starship Elysian Dawn.

Seventeen elite adventurers, as their employers dub them, enter the simulation. Harry finds them a mixed bunch indeed. He is a physician, but the others range from a teenage acrobat and a midwife to a geologist, and from a vet and a game developer to an expert in ancient history. The one who intrigues Harry is Rachel Traveller, a nutritionist with a peculiar ability she calls clearsight.

As the group work through the challenges of simulation, isolation, and spending time in a stasis-tank, their numbers dwindle until just two of them are left. Now Harry and Rachel prepare for the final challenge, after which they'll be ready to board the starship.

Meanwhile, the Outward Bound company faces changing times and goalpost challenges, and some of these might have alarming consequences for Harry and his plans.

Rachel Outward Bound
Copyright © 2024 Sally Odgers
ISBN: 978-1-4874-4269-9
Cover art by Martine Jardin

Published by eXtasy Books Inc

Look for us online at:
www.eXtasybooks.com

Rachel Outward Bound
Elydian Dawn 4

By

Sally Odgers

DEDICATION

For everyone who has suffered from shifting goalposts

Author's Note

When the starship *Elysian Dawn* crash-landed eighteen years into its journey, a rescue mission was mounted. One of the rescue team was Doctor Harry Fejoa, a specialist in exotic diseases and mental health. Harry's story was at least as strange as Marianne Arcadia's, which is told in *Elysian Dawn, The Silvering,* and *New Dreams,* though for very different reasons.

Rachel Outward Bound begins in 2232, forty years before the crash. This story takes place mostly on Terra and introduces younger versions of familiar characters including Harry Fejoa, Landon Chavez, Cornelia Conti, Samantha Woo, Tomas Ash, and Harley Neal.

CHAPTER ONE: POTENTIALITY, GREATER SOUTHERN: 2232

Name: Harry Fejoa
DOB: 25-11-2207
POB: Greater Southern
Ethnicity: Euro-Greater Southern 60%
Qualifications: Physician: specialising in exotic diseases and counselling
N.O.K.: Flavia Neal

After those common-or-garden questions came the rabble. *Height-weight-religion-orientation-personality-type*

Harry filled them in with his hand on autopilot. His mind was busy asking itself why it had to be done by hand. Had these people never heard of voca-forms? They'd been around for long enough to lose their capital letter and become a generic noun.

Most of what he wrote was true — the checkable stuff, anyway. His qualifications were a matter of record, and the so-called *status quo* factors were encoded in the chip in his wrist. Anyone could check his veracity on those with a handshake — or a high-five — or even an avuncular pat on the wrist.

Flav might be astonished to find herself tagged as his next-of-kin, but she wouldn't object. They were third cousins, he thought, and she was the kindest person he knew. She was fifteen years older than Harry, but she had always made time for him when he needed a friend, advice, or anything she could offer, really. She'd been his graduation date, beaming with genuine pride that *wee Hazzy* — the name she had chosen when he was fourteen and she thought he needed taking down a few pegs — was now Doctor Harry Fejoa. In turn, he was godfather to her only child. He had closer blood-ties than Flav and Harley, but none he cared to acknowledge.

He slid the datasheet into the slot provided and touched his wrist to the screen to verify his identity.

You've got an identity-screener. Where's the voca-form?

After that, he waited.

The room he was in was really more of a cubical. It had a water spigot, a toilet closet, and a small food dispensary. It had nothing for entertainment unless he took up toilet-paper origami.

Harry supposed that was deliberate. He had no doubt someone, whether human or AI or somewhere in between, was monitoring him. That was just mean.

There was no clock and he hadn't been allowed to bring in any personal electronics, books, paper or writing implements. They'd confiscated his knitting. Fair enough, Harry thought. He'd been pulling their chains on that one.

The stylus would write only on the datasheet, which was now out of reach.

Harry, after an unimpressed once-over of the cubical, put himself into a light trance. Time passed, giving the impression of a time-lapse animation. He watched imaginary clouds speeding through sunsets.

The door opened and a man came in. He had a high-bridged nose, dark eyes, and a mulish mouth. He looked to be at least forty-five, but Harry thought he was almost certainly younger. Some people, in his experience, aged unexpectedly, either looking youthful well into middle age or scowling their way to maturity and beyond when still in their twenties.

Harry didn't like the anomaly, but he brought himself to

full consciousness in less than the snap of his fingers. It wasn't necessarily the man's fault he was out of chronological step with himself.

The man sat down on an armed chair facing Harry and looked at him.

Harry looked back.

"So," the man said, "why would someone like you want to work for Outward Bound?"

Harry said, in italics and with false enthusiasm, "*Are you ready for the adventure of a lifetime?*" He did jazz hands a couple of times for emphasis and rolled his eyes for effect before his eyebrows went into manic overdrive.

"Ah, so you saw one of our ad-banners."

"I assumed they were meant to be seen," Harry said cordially.

"Ye-es."

"You sound uncertain."

"Fewer than a quarter of a percent of people have seen one. Most of those who do don't act on what they see."

"Subliminal advertising?" Harry suggested.

The man smiled scornfully. "That theory was disproved a long time ago."

"That doesn't mean it doesn't work."

"It wasn't subliminal advertising."

"What, then?"

The man leaned forward, his large, bumpy-knuckled hands clasping the arms of the chair. A sewn badge rippled under the strip lighting and his name briefly flashed to visibility. *L. Chavez.* "It's called *potentiality*. I don't know the details, but I'm told it's based on coded patterns that the brains of certain people can unscramble."

"So, you were looking for someone who could read those words."

"Not *those* words. No. Not those particular words. With

potentiality, people see — if they see anything — something their brains configure. In short, they see the message they expect — or fear, or want — to see."

"Expect, in my case," Harry said.

"Ah?"

"I *expected* to see a banal baited hook. I didn't want to and I'm not afraid of anything."

Chavez looked sceptical. "That's a rash statement."

"No, why? Fear is a human response intended to keep us safe. Fear keeps us from jumping off Great Southern Bridge. I'm not afraid because I'm not suicidal. Fear of what *I* might do means not trusting myself. Fear of what others might do is immaterial. I can't foresee or control it, so it serves no useful purpose."

"An interesting point of view."

"Logical, I'd say. Fear is useful only in as much as it allows us to avoid danger. Mostly, when a man walks into danger it's due to something he can't expect or else his own stupidity."

Chavez leaned forward a bit more. "What did you want to see, Doctor Fejoa?"

"Something interesting."

Chavez nodded. "I repeat, why would someone like you want to work for Outward Bound?"

"I want to travel, but not without purpose and meaning. I trained as a doctor of the body and mind. I am interested in how human bodies and minds respond to the challenge of the unexpected and the unknowable." He paused for a beat, and added, "And what do you mean by *a person like me*?"

"I meant you have an entrepreneurial personality type. You're a decider. A leader. That means you should want to establish yourself in your own canoe, not paddle in someone else's."

"One might suppose so," Harry said.

4

"So why don't you?"

"I don't have the financial freedom to build my own canoe."

"You're intelligent enough to subvert the system."

"Unfortunately, I also have ethics."

"I see. What do you know about Outward Bound?"

"About as much as most people. It's a company that looks out and up rather than back and inward. You're building a starship."

Chavez held up one hand. "A colony ship."

"A colony ship going to the stars."

Chavez touched a button in the arm of his chair. A holographic screen sprang out, showing the blueprints of a spaceship. It wasn't immediately prepossessing, lacking tapers, sleek lines, and graceful proportions.

Harry felt a second of regret for the lost beauty of the past. *San Felipe* of 1690. *Golden Hind* of 1570. *Endeavour* of 1774.

"This is *Elysian Dawn*," Chavez said. He waited a beat and added, "I should say, this *will* be *Elysian Dawn*. Once built, she will carry a payload of colonists-elect to Magellan Sixteen."

Harry felt his brows go up in surprise. "That far!"

"What did you expect?"

"The closer extra-Sol planets first."

"None is particularly suited to our needs. Terraforming is expensive and may fail. Magellan Sixteen is a planet in the Goldilocks Zone, very like Terra."

Harry said, "I didn't know scouts had gone out that far."

"They haven't."

"So, launch is a long way in the future."

"We are looking at twenty years maximum," Chavez said. "That gives us time to perfect the FeTtL drive which is in the late testing phase, to build the ship, and to select colonists elect. It also allows the current Outward Bound board to oversee the project from blueprint to launch — barring accidents."

"I'll be forty-five in twenty years. Will that be a problem?"

A strange expression crossed Chavez's face.

Ah, you'll be older still, Harry thought. Or maybe you lack the drive to travel on your huge canoe. He said, abruptly, "How long will the trip be? Assuming it's one-way?"

"Why do you ask?"

"I'm trying to work out the logistics of having a trained crew who will be young enough to—but of course, you can't, can you? Going that far, even with FeTtL drive, it's going to take decades to get out to Magellan."

"Centuries," Chavez said. "If you look at it one way."

Harry waited.

Chavez said, "Have you heard of the stasis-tank system?"

"Yes."

"That does surprise me."

"It shouldn't. It's used for trauma victims, and there's also considerable interest in employing it for cure-coasting. Not that anyone's tried so far. Not successfully."

"And why's that?" Chavez sounded no more than mildly interested.

Harry wanted to frown. He disliked being played, and he was certain Chavez was a player. Still, he answered equably.

"The trauma tanks work for subjects by taking the onus off their bodies and minds. Floating in bio-equality-stasis-sustainability-environmental-fluid allows bodies to heal, and the sensory deprivation calms the brain waves. However, participants remain in a hypnotic state where they are aware—distantly—of their surroundings. Cure-coasting—waiting in quasi-status until a cure can be developed or a genetic match found—would by definition mean an extended period and too long in the hypno-state—" He broke off. "You already know all this."

"I know that's the current belief," Chavez said. He sounded distant, amused—and smug.

6

Harry liked him less.

"What would you say if I suggested a new generation sta-sis-tank system has the potential to keep humans — any life form, for that matter — in stas for a century or more?"

"I'd ask who fed you that twaddle."

"It's true."

"Stas isn't suspended animation," Harry snapped.

"No, but the bio-fluid can be altered to slow its guests — "

"Guests?"

"It acts as a host, so why not? The guest is not in suspension, but slowed enormously, so it ages approximately one day for every year. At least, that's the theory."

Harry let that simmer for half a second. Then he said, "You're planning to tank your colonists."

"Obviously," Chavez said. "How else could they survive to reach Magellan Sixteen?"

How else indeed.

Harry riposted, "I doubt you'll find many colonists-elect willing to sleep in a tank for centuries with no guarantee of waking safely — or at all."

A vaguely shark-like smile spread over Chavez' face for a blink before it was gone. "That, Doctor Fejoa, is why we are running tank tests now. If we can demonstrate the viability of the tank system over several years, that will negate — "

Harry snorted.

"Of course there is some risk for our volunteers," Chavez continued. "That's why we offer financial enticements — among other things — to early-uptake participants."

Harry gave the man a mental slow handclap. "Oh, very *good*," he said warmly. "I doubt if a financial enticement is much use to someone who is asleep with no guarantee of waking. As a matter of interest, how *does* that work? Do you offer the enticement to be enjoyed for — say — ten years before stuffing your victim in the tank?"

"No. There's a good chance the participant would renege. We offer shares in Outward Bound, a guaranteed place in *Elysian Dawn* if the participant chooses to take it, and a large stipend which, should things go wrong, will still be paid to the participant's designated heir."

Flavia's face flashed through Harry's mind. Flav was a nice woman. She was kind and helpful. She worked hard and yet—she was unlucky. People said money didn't bring happiness, but Harry knew from observation that lack of it did bring unhappiness. Little Harley was the light of Flav's life, and he knew how much it hurt her that Harley would lack the chances life offered to the golden spoons of society.

He was too newly qualified to have made any dent in his huge education debt, but he'd always promised himself he'd help Flav if he were ever in the position to do so.

"How much are we talking?" he asked.

"In dollar terms, it's a meaningless concept. There's no use for money in space. However, it's enough to set the participant up for life if she or he remains on Terra."

"And if she or he chooses to go *outward bound*? Or dies? Or is refused travel? What happens to the generous stipend then?"

"Then the funds will go to the nominated heir. So, Doctor Fejoa. Are you interested?"

"Interested, yes. Committed, no. How many people do you have signed up so far?"

"None as yet. As I said, few see the banner-ad and fewer still act on it. Only a tiny percentage of those who do will be selected."

"And what's the plan? Will you be fielding hundreds or thousands and training them? You'd need a huge pool of applicants."

"Initially, we mean to choose twenty participants. The schedule is as follows."

Chavez dismissed the blueprint and brought up a timeline. "As you see, the first twenty will enter a simulation habitat where they will spend a year studying, working, and experiencing isolation from normal social parameters. At the end of the sim, there will be a review and debriefing. Anyone who is deemed unfit for long-haul space travel and dislocation from Terran life will be paid off. The remainder will enter the stastanks for a period of five hours. Again there will be a review and debriefing. The next round will be a few days in the tanks, then a month. After that—"

"The lucky few survivors get their wings?"

Chavez shook his head. "After that, we will call for volunteers to put in an extended period in stas."

"Two months?"

"Five years."

Harry whistled. "What's next—ten years?"

"No. Five seems a fair enough test. By then, *Elysian Dawn* may be nearing completion and intensive training can begin."

"If you start with twenty and end up with . . . oh, six or so . . . that will *not* be a viable sample."

Chavez sighed. "During the test period of the early-adopters, we will be choosing and training the rest of the colonists-elect from a much wider pool. They will be ready for when the elite adventurers wake from the five-year stas."

"If they wake."

"We have no reason to believe they won't. A few hours, a few days . . . the process is much the same."

"Tell that to frozen beans." Harry rose to his feet. "Thank you for this most enlightening discussion, Mister Chavez. I wish you and your company well."

He had the pleasure of seeing a disconcerted expression slide over the man's arrogant features.

"You're leaving?"

"Mister Chavez, anyone who signed up for this exercise in

craziness would be certifiably nuts and probably suicidal. The type of person who plays chicken with the super-trains and wears boots with anti-fric heels."

"And that's your professional opinion."

"It is," Harry said cordially. "How does one get out of this place?"

For a wild moment he wondered what he would do if Chavez did a certifiably nuts cackle and said, *You don't.*

Instead, the man rose and held out a stiff hand. "Through that door. Someone will show you out. Thank you for your time, Doctor Fejoa."

Harry sighed and sat down. "So, maybe I *am* certifiably nuts though not suicidal. Where's this simulation?"

CHAPTER TWO: DICE, 2233

While Harry waited for the simulation to come online, he worked for Outward Bound.

Chavez employed him as a recruiter, having him run silent psyche tests on the subjects who came to apply, to query, or just to satisfy their curiosity. When Harry questioned the ethics of this, Chavez said the subjects' presence at Outward Bound's recruitment office could be taken as tacit agreement to any screening process the board deemed necessary.

"If it makes you feel better, we can add that to the application form, along with the normal NDA," he said.

"Do that, or I walk." Harry wondered what else Chavez thought was tacitly agreed. "I suppose you're aware I haven't signed an NDA myself," he added in a mild tone that might be construed as a threat if Chavez chose.

"Then you'll do it now." Chavez clicked up one of his holograms and posted an agreement.

Harry read it through at an unnecessarily slow speed, as proof he intended to understand what he was signing. *I agree not to speak of, write, disclose, or otherwise dissemble anything I shall learn while employed by Outward Bound.*

He blew out his cheeks in a silent and private sigh of relief. The modal verb made all the difference. He couldn't speak of anything *new* he learned, but he reckoned he was ethically free to mention anything he'd learned or surmised already. *They should have written it as "anything I have learned, surmised or been told, and anything I shall learn surmise or be told in future." And there should have been a rider to add "either during my employment or at any later date."*

Whoever had written the thing didn't understand the power of words.

He signed, using his wrist chip.

Working for Outward Bound proved mostly interesting, sometimes tedious, and rather claustrophobic. Harry wasn't obliged to stay at the facility full time, but he was *on call,* a euphemism and an excuse to track his movements.

He had no strong objection to this. He understood Outward Bound needed its subjects and employees to be committed. Besides, he wasn't going anywhere to trouble them.

He made the occasional visit to Flavia and Harley Neal as he always had, work and study permitting. Harley was too young to ask questions, and he told Flavia only that he had picked up full-time though not permanent work for a company who wanted to psych-screen applicants for positions.

It was true enough.

He didn't tell Flavia he had made her his heir. That would have prompted questions and troubled her.

Months later, he took his usual seat at the one-way window into the cubicle where one of Chavez's colleagues, Cataleya Conti, patiently interviewed a subject. Conti was a middle-aged woman of startling ordinariness. Harry thought that unfortunate. Someone named Cataleya Conti should be exotic and probably equipped with camellias or castanets. This one was sallow, with long mousy hair in a bun and insignificant hips and breasts. She had nice eyes, but otherwise she was so determinedly plain and unremarkable he was sure she was doing it on purpose. Now — why? He'd pondered this off and on since their first encounter and hadn't come to any clear conclusion. He was tempted to invite her to dinner to find out. He was sure she wouldn't take it for anything other than the fishing trip it was. She was older than Flav and much more forgettable.

He pried his attention loose from Conti and her possible motives and applied it to her interviewee instead. He sat silently observing until the subject was thanked and sent to the company canteen for refreshments "while I run the algorithms."

When the door closed behind the subject, Conti looked straight at the window and cocked her head.

That was Harry's cue. He let himself into the cubicle.

Conti gave him her quick on-off smile. "What do you think, Doctor Algorithm?"

"That one's running," he said.

"Damn."

"Sorry." He grimaced. "You know, you could do worse than to take some runners. It would be charitable."

She gave a tiny headshake. "I see your point—no, I do, truly—but victims are victims, on this world or any other. Victims have no chance out in the wild."

"You can't blame victims for the bullies of this world."

"I don't. But we all have bullies, Doctor Fejoa. *All* of us. It's how we deal with them that forms our destiny. Some run, some fight, some sidestep, and some just get on with life by ignoring the provocation."

"It's not as simple as that."

"It has to be—otherwise we'd have a payload of inadequate people, and we *can't*."

"You don't mince your words."

She lifted her chin. He was reminded of a sparrow squaring up to a hawk.

Maybe he *would* ask her to dinner. He couldn't afford to take her out formally, but walking by the river was free, and a French stick, cheese, and grapes could pass for intentionally quaint. His pay for the psych work was reasonable, but most of it went on his riverside apartment. After a day in the confines of the cubby, he needed space and peace to air out his mind.

"You wouldn't want to share a new world with inadequate people," he agreed. He added, "but look on the brighter side. As a member of the selection committee, you can choose at least some people you find compatible."

"Compatible with whom?"

"With yourself."

"But I never do find people compatible. I prefer spaniels. They're demanding but congenial."

"I wonder if there will be spaniels on Magellan Sixteen." He knew they were taking goats and ducks and possibly horses.

"It won't concern me. I'll be long gone before *Elysian Dawn* is even halfway there."

"You're not travelling?" He had assumed she would.

"Of course not." She met his gaze. "Why would you think I'd be selected? I'm much too old. Besides, I'm at least as inadequate as the people I'm turning down."

"You're not a runner," he said. "I can't imagine you running from anyone or anything."

"I don't run away from life, but I don't run *to* it, either. I just keep my head down and paddle like mad in the status quo. Thanks for the reading." She looked above his head. "There's the ping. The next bunny's waiting."

Harry had intended to continue the conversation, but he found himself returning to his cubbyhole. He wondered who Conti was really, and whether her subdued clothing, unbecoming hairstyle, and understated manner were disguise or armour or neither. Possibly, they were camouflage.

He suddenly looked forward to finding out, but the next day Bindilina Ash was the interviewer, then Bao Woo, with his serene smile and square cut black hair, and after that it was Chavez again. Others of the company took their turns, but these were the four he saw most often. He knew they were all board-members, and he'd noted that Chavez, although probably the youngest, acted as a functional leader, though he doubted if that was officially sanctioned.

"A word," Chavez said at the end of one especially long day.

Harry waited to be castigated for shaking his head over nineteen of the twenty applicants of the day. He had his reasons ready. Many of them were runners. He sympathised with them, but Conti was right. If they couldn't live bravely and capably on Terra they would be just as dysfunctional on a starship. Could one be dysfunctional while sleeping in a tank? They'd be dysfunctional on Magellan Sixteen, he amended.

Of those who weren't running from their lives, some were motivated by greed — not for wealth but for position. These saw themselves as colony leaders and lawgivers, never as worker ants. Then there were the hopeless, those who knew, or believed, they could never get anywhere in their current lives. They wanted a way out, and shipping out in a tank was slightly less final than suicide.

We need the capable. The can-do. The innovators. Failing that, we need people who could be all of the above if they had a fighting chance.

He had these reasons on his tongue, but Chavez said abruptly, "The sim's ready. You and the other elites enter it tomorrow morning."

Harry prided himself on not being easily surprised, but this news shook him.

"I thought that was still six months away."

"Tomorrow." Chavez gave him a slanting glance. "I hope that gives you enough notice to arrange your affairs."

Harry divined the man hoped and expected it wouldn't, so he nodded phlegmatically. "Oh yes. And I trust the sim funds will be in my nominated account *before* I enter."

"Yes."

"So I can draw some out to prepay my rent."

"They will be in the holding account," Chavez corrected. "They will be released to you after the trials if you elect not to ship out or to your heir should things not go to plan."

"If I die in the sim."

"There's no reason to think you will die in the sim. Safest place in the world."

"I'm sure it is. Until it isn't." Harry nodded. "But that's not good enough, Chavez. I want some of those funds released to my heir immediately. She will pay my rent and such."

"The agreement—"

"Damn the agreement." Harry tossed his dice. "All being well, I might live another seventy years. I'm spending the next several years at your beck and call and after we enter stas on the ship, I will have no use for money. I want one seventieth of those funds released now, for my heir to use on my behalf while I'm in the sim." He held the other man's gaze, betting that his proven usefulness so far would make Chavez reluctant to lose him.

Chavez nodded. "Done. It will be in your nominated account as soon as you enter the sim. But you should terminate your apartment. There's no point keeping it empty for a year, and after that year, if you make the cut, you'll remain at the sim campus for the tank tests."

"There will be time between those."

"You will be working on the *Elysian Dawn* project and your day-to-day life on Terra will no longer exist."

"I see." Harry gave Chavez an insincere smile. "Then I'd better go and sort out my apartment. And for that, I need those funds. There will be a cash-out penalty. If you had given me a month's notice, that wouldn't have been the case."

"The funds will be released immediately."

Harry nodded and walked out.

As he made the half-hour journey to his riverside

apartment, he wondered how angry he should be and whether Chavez was to be trusted. He'd given in suspiciously easily.

Mind games. Or maybe it's another personality test. Counsellor, counsel thyself.

You signed up for this, he reminded himself.

About to enter his domain and work out what he needed to store for a year and where to store it, he abruptly changed his mind and caught the zip into the city instead. He had no need to store anything. Whatever happened his general life was over. Chavez was right about that. If he survived the sim — and again Chavez was right to say it wasn't dangerous unless one was overly extrovert or claustrophobic — and the tank tests, which were much riskier, then he'd eventually be leaving old Terra forever. Dead or among the stars. What a choice.

Chapter Three: Flavia, 2233

The Pleasant View Estate was a lie thrice over. It wasn't pleasant, there was no view, and it wasn't an estate. It was a vast apartment complex built to a plan that packed more people per square kilometre than had ever been possible before. Walls were thin, ceilings were low, and doors were flimsy.

They wouldn't stop a determined ten-year-old, but then, as the inhabitants sometimes quipped, no one who lived behind them had anything worth stealing.

Harry navigated through the narrow passageways of the grid until he came to Apt.19-4-H.

He touched his wrist chip to the grid on the door.

A few seconds later, the door buzzed and opened.

Harry walked in, ducking through the inadequate space.

"Hazzy!" Harley, clad in a turquoise shirt over brief pants, grabbed him around the knees. He staggered, then bent to lift the child into his arms.

"Boo!"

Harley squealed and hugged him.

"Ugh, you're sticky," Harry said, looking down into her smiling eyes, confusingly, of different colours. One was dark, sapphire blue like her mother's. The other was green hazel on one side and paler blue on the other.

"She's always sticky," Flavia said, coming through from the second room. "How are you, Harry?"

"Better than you I expect," he said.

Flavia was forty-one, but she looked older, tired, and

defeated.

"I'm fine."

"You don't look it."

"Harry, you're a counsellor. You're supposed to reassure your clients not to make them doubt themselves."

"You're not my client." He kissed Harley's cheek. "Uh, Turq. You seriously need a bath." Then he looked at Flavia again. "Water trouble?"

She shrugged. "Not more than usual."

"How many days has it been off this time?"

"It's not off. Just pressured down."

"How bad?"

"Stop it, Harry. We manage."

Yes, he thought, by leaving a bucket under a tap left running all day.

"You shouldn't have to manage. You should—"

"Should won't butter any buns."

"No, but *I* can!" Harry put the child down and fished some pats of butter out of his pack. "There's some cheese, too, and those little biscuits. Here." He upended the pack on the low table. "There you are, Turq. Dig in." He met Flavia's gaze. "I wanted to bring fruit, but this is all I could get. They feed us mainly on soup and that's not very transportable."

"Believe me, we're grateful for this." Flavia watched Harley bite a hole in the cheese wrapping and blissfully suck on the contents.

"That kid's a grub," Harry said.

"All kids are grubs. It's part of the product description. How's work? Are you still doing psych checks for that company?"

"That's finished. I start a new job tomorrow. Same company, different branch. And—better pay."

"That's great."

"The downside is I won't be around to see you for a while."

"You have no obligation to see us."

"What a whopper! That sticky-ite is my godchild!"

"Yes, but we always knew you could be transferred at any time. Medical staff go where they're needed."

"Not going to ask me how long?"

"How long?" she asked obligingly.

"A year. And after that I'll be doing something else which might make it difficult to come here, or anywhere. Sit down, Flav. I've got things to tell you."

"That sounds ominous." She sat on the low chair and Harry perched on a crate that had once held potatoes.

"It is a bit. Flav, have you ever heard of Outward Bound?"

She frowned. "I think so—are they the ones building the starship?"

"That's right."

"What about them?"

"That's the company I work for. They're the ones doing the interviews for colonists and crew. I listen in and perform silent psych checks."

"Silent, eh?" She wrinkled her nose with distaste.

Harry didn't blame her.

He told Flavia briefly what he'd learned and surmised over his months of working for Outward Bound. "You understand this is absolutely under the rose."

Flavia nodded and crossed her heart. Her face was pale already, but it blanched as she took in the enormity of what he said. "You're going on this starship."

"I am, yes, if I get through the sim and survive the tank tests. And there's no reason to think I won't. They've already tanked animals for a few weeks with no ill effects."

"I hadn't heard that."

"It's not common knowledge. Anyway, it won't be for a while yet, but I'll be kept busy, and I have the feeling I'll be gently dissuaded from wandering away in case I break my

NDA."

"As if you would."

"As if I would. Obviously, Flav, I'm not supposed to talk about this, but it concerns you and Turq. I want you to apply for a place on the ship."

Flavia said, flatly, "I can't possibly. I have no talents and no useful attributes."

"You have Turq. She's exactly the sort of person who should go on Outward Bound's great adventure. But Flav, don't apply yet. Wait until I finish the sim and the tests and can be sure it's viable. In the meanwhile, I'll talk you through the application, so you'll make the cut. The main thing is to emphasise the positives. Talk up adventure, pioneering, and so on. Don't even suggest you're running from anything."

She shook her head. "Harry, it can't happen. Harley might go, but by the time this ship leaves I'll be nearly sixty."

"So?"

She looked down at her hands. "Colonies need children."

"You have a child."

"She'll be emancipated by then. No. Please, Harry. Forget it. Forget us. Go and live your life. You don't owe us anything."

Harry closed his eyes for a few seconds. When he looked back at her he said, "I thought you might say that, but I had to tell you. Flav, will you marry me?"

Her eyes widened and she yelped and lifted a hand to her mouth. "Ow . . . bit my tongue! Hazzy, don't be such a—no. No, I won't. It's inappropriate. Besides, I'm already married."

"Dissolve it."

"I can't. I don't know where he is, and it's better that way. He's red-chipped. Applying for a dissolution means tracking him down, which would just attract his attention."

"I thought you might say that, too—though I didn't know you and Turq's father were formal. Okay, here's my third and final suggestion. I'm being paid well to enter this sim and to do the tanking tests. I've persuaded the board—or the representative I report to most often—to release a portion of the funds before I go dark. I'm making that over to you." He held up his hand to forestall her protest. "You're my next-of-kin and this is one way I can make life a bit better for you and Turq. No, *listen.* I've been told to relinquish my apartment but to do that without notice will bring a penalty with it. It would be better, economically speaking, if you and Turq take it over. It's designated for one adult occupant, but you'd be able to stay until the grub hits emancipation age.

"If you prefer to stay at Pleasant View, I'll pay the penalty of relinquishment and transfer the rest of the funds to you." He cocked an eyebrow. "Want the apartment or not?"

"Yes," she said.

"Good. I hate to waste good funds on a penalty. I haven't time to clear my stuff out, so I'm leaving that to you. Do what you want with it. I was going to store it, but there's no point."

"You said you weren't leaving yet," she put in.

"I know, but from what's been said, and what hasn't, I think we have to wind up our lives here before we move on." He took her hand and gave it a squeeze. "Flav, I might be able to visit sometimes, or not. I think we'll say not, but if I turn up one day, I hope you'll butter a bun for me."

Flavia opened her mouth a couple of times, but nothing came out.

"You can move in tomorrow after I leave or spend as long as you like sorting things out here first. Is there a penalty for leaving here without notice?"

"I don't know. People often do leave unexpectedly."

"You sort it out then. I'll give you the door code."

He touched his wrist chip to hers and transferred the code. "There. You'll be able to get in. Now . . . " He let go her hand and double-tapped his wrist. "Good. The funds are in." He took her hand again and made the transfer. "Right—that will last for a while. In the meantime, you could apply to Outward Bound as a worker if you won't sign up to travel. I might be able to swing something." He bent and kissed her cheek. "Bye, Flav. And Turq—" He scooped up the child, who had managed to get cheese in her hair. "You seriously have to have a bath, Turq."

He gave her a hug and left.

His dice had given him a double six.

Chapter Four: Rachel, 2233

Harry entered the sim the morning after his visit to Flavia and Harley.

It bothered him that he might never see them again, but as Flavia said, they'd always known he could be transferred anywhere at any time without notice.

Medics weren't supposed to have private lives. They were supposed to dedicate themselves to others.

Harry's conscience was clear as he stood naked in a decon cubicle. He didn't know where he was, geographically speaking. He'd been anesthetised and transported somewhere. Here. It was ridiculously cloak-and-dagger. What would it matter if he knew where he was?

Shipping out on *Elysian Dawn* didn't mean shipping out of his responsibilities. His skills and qualifications would be needed on Magellan Sixteen. No matter how carefully screened the settlers were, inevitably some of them would become homesick and regret their decision to ship out. They would all be told, repeatedly, that this was a one-way journey, but they probably wouldn't internalise that fact until it was too late. Even if the starship were capable of making a return to Terra, and Harry honestly didn't know if it was, it would still be impossible to *come back.*

Harry remembered 2217 — he'd been ten years old — but no amount of remembering could take him back there.

That wouldn't be the whole of it, either. If anyone became seriously ill, which could happen despite genetic screening, they and their fellow settlers would have to accept probable premature death. Medical skills and knowledge could be carried to a new world, but the health infrastructure, built over centuries, could not.

Even encyclopaedic medical knowledge might be of little use if Magellan Sixteen had diseases compatible with the human host. It was said that even a mild disease could kill if it had a close encounter with someone who had no acquired immunity.

On the shoulders of giants was an apt saying. The physical giants of hospitals and vast resources would be left behind.

The cubicle lit with blue light and Harry raised his arms and turned slowly as instructed.

The instructions were his. One of his specialities was exotic diseases, and although he rarely encountered any, he knew the protocols. *Isolate, irradiate, eradicate,* as the saying went, though *irradiate* was going a step too far.

Harry didn't have any diseases, let alone exotic ones, but anyone who entered the sim had to be free of pathogens. It was agreed there would be no rescue from outside and no communication until the year was up.

That meant spending a dull and uncomfortable seven days in an isolation decon cubicle, breathing filtered air, drinking sterilised water, and swallowing a vile concoction that supplied nutrients and antibiotics while rigorously purging all traces of meals consumed beforehand. It purged gut flora too but reinstated a new version that approximated what scientists thought might be prevalent on Magellan Sixteen.

It was very like the way infestations of exotic amoeba or yeasts were treated. Effectively, they were rinsed and starved, then jettisoned through natural channels.

Harry felt like the Augean stables.

The blue light prickled.

He wanted to scrub his hands over his sides, but he went on holding out his arms, reciting periodic tables to take his mind off the discomfort.

This is ridiculous. They can't replicate life on Magellan Sixteen. They don't know what it's like, except theoretically. It's a sim. We all know it's a sim. There's no need for all this.

A glass of thick liquid, too cool to be a hot drink and too warm to be cold, rose from a dispenser.

Harry drank it, grimacing at the taste as well as the knowledge of what it would shortly be doing to his body.

Toilet. Now.

Blue light.

Drink.

Toilet. Now.

Blue light . . .

Ugh. He wished he'd never seen that banner-ad.

The constant temperature and light messed with his circadian rhythms. The silence messed with his mind. This was all expected. He knew he had to be dismantled, sort of, before he could begin life in the sim. All the discomforts of having his bodily and mental habits disrupted had to happen before the sim.

Blue light.

Drink.

Toilet. Now.

Harry told the blue light what he thought of it.

A white bulb lit in the corner of the cubicle. Below it, a screen slid out of the wall and printed words. *To end decontamination and to exit the program tap screen twice.*

What the hell?

Harry turned his back on the screen. He hadn't known there was a way out.

It occurred to him that someone, possibly Chavez, might be sitting behind a one-way window watching his discomfort.

To end decontamination and to exit the program tap screen twice.

Did that mean his seven days were finished? Would tapping twice move him on into the sim? Or would it eject him prematurely, washing him out of the program?

He rolled his eyes. Why hadn't they hired someone with word sense to write these damned instructions?

He turned back and tapped the screen once.

The screen faded and reformed. *Exit program prematurely? This cannot be undone.*

That was clear enough, except there was no way to say *no.* Presumably one tapped for a second time to say *yes.*

Harry told the screen what he thought of its ineptitude.

It retreated.

Blue light.

Drink.

"Not bloody likely," Harry said. "There's nothing left in my intestines but the lining and probably that's not in good shape."

The sludge in the glass drained away. The glass retreated.

Blue light.

Drink. This time, the liquid was clear.

Harry sipped cautiously. Water.

Toilet. Right now.

Water and an undetectable laxative, he told himself. *Creeps.*

By the time the program finished and the cramping eased, he felt weak and transparent.

A pair of shorts and a shirt dropped from the ceiling hatch.

From the lack of smell and colour, he decided these had also been subjected to the blue light and might shortly fall apart.

He showered in suspiciously blue water, was dried by a warm gush of aggressively filtered air, and prompted to clothe himself.

He did so.

After that, the cubicle door opened, and he walked out into a large room that was subtly wrong.

It was empty but for basic furniture. A French door led out into a bland outdoor setting with trees, flowers, rocks, and grass, also subtly wrong.

The light was odd, and perspective looked uneven.

Harry looked at the sky and perceived a shimmering dome.

This must be the habitat.

He told the habitat what he thought of it.

His stomach lurched. He thought he might have thrown up if there had been anything in his body to throw.

Someone laughed.

Harry turned.

The woman facing him was young, with dark hair cut close to her head and skin that looked as if it should be a warm olive. After a week of blue light and decontamination, it looked drab. She had on the same type of clothing as his— shorts and a shirt of an indeterminate colour. Fortnight-old porridge was the kindest comparison he could come up with. She looked gaunt, but recently so. He supposed he looked no better.

"Hello," he said.

"Hello." She paused and added, "What you said."

"Emoting is healthy. The way we've been treated is not de-signed to be taken lying down."

"I did, most of the time." She laid her hand on her stomach. "Concave. Women's stomachs are not meant to be concave."

"No one is meant to be concave. Harry Fejoa."

"I know."

"How?"

"You sat in on my initial interview. You were lurking be-hind a window contraption, but I saw you."

"How? That's a one-way window."

"I have hyper focus. That's the official description. *I* call it *clearsight*. I asked about you, casually, and described you. Someone said you were a mind-doctor. Is sympathy in or-der?"

"What?"

"You must have done something terrible to be chucked in here with the crazies."

"Elite subjects," he reproved. "I'm one of you."

"How odd. Did you sit in on your own initial interview and sort through your own psyche?"

"I was present at my interview, obviously. I don't know who, if anyone, sorted through my psyche." He frowned. "I think I was one of the first respondents. Maybe *the* first to get an interview."

"Could be. I'm Rachel Traveller. And yes, it's my real, original name." She spread her hands. "So you see, I had no choice. I had to join the crazies."

"You believe in the influence of names?"

"Don't you?"

"I think our names influence us, but we also influence them. If a name is doing us no favours, we should change it."

"How rude. Our names are a gift from our caregivers, and from history," she scolded.

Harry said, "Life is made up of things we can't change along with a few we can. It's our right to change what we can if that's to our advantage."

"Even if it disappoints other people?"

He shrugged. "Honour thy father and mother? Maybe I would if they were still around. They left me with friends while they went on a couples-only holiday. They died in a smash on the way to the airport. I was an obnoxious child. Just as well, or they'd have taken me along on a family week instead of choosing couples-only and I'd have died too."

"Mine aren't around either. Clearsight made me an anomaly, and my childish prattle about what I saw was embarrassing, so they handed me over to the white coats to be deprogrammed."

"It didn't work."

She favoured him with a fiendish smile. "Did you change your name to become a green fruit?"

"No. It's a different spelling. I've never met anyone else with the same name, apart from my lamented parents. I suspect Dad's family was from Angola originally and he modified the spelling for some reason." He remembered his thoughts on Cataleya Conti's name and wondered if his did him any favours. He concluded it did. *Harry Fejoa* had a carefree ring, even if the spelling was unusual. Even if it made a fellow elite classify him as a green fruit.

As he thought about it, another portion of his mind was flipping through mental files to find Rachel Traveller. He'd not had names provided, but he thought she'd come up as Number Twenty-seven—early enough in the program to be memorable. At that point there were three or four subjects a day. Later, it had been nearer to thirty.

"You were wearing a khaki shirt," he said.

She nodded. "I wanted to look earnest and worthy. A new world has no place for creatures of vain adornment."

"If that were so, Cataleya Conti would be the perfect candidate," he said.

Up went her brows. "She's not going? I thought she would be."

"No. Neither are Chavez, Bao Woo, or Bindilina Ash."

"Then what's in it for them?"

"Scientific curiosity, humanitarian ideals, a desire to play puppet master, vicarious excitement—take your pick." He smiled and said, "They're in an anomalous position, spending a large portion of their lives preparing for a great adventure."

"We're in the same situation."

"You know that isn't so."

She sighed. "Yes, I know. We'll enter the stas pods and eventually wake to start a new life, but they'll never have that execution of their dreams. They're preparing the adventure for other people."

Harry said soberly, "They'll age and die, knowing we're out there, but they won't know what will happen when we arrive and there will be no live communication on the way."

"I suppose not. They'll have instruments monitoring the ship, but they won't be able to do anything to influence it, and none of us will be able to report. They'll never know if the dice rolls a six or falls through a crack in the table."

That's odd, Harry thought. He'd had notions of dice himself.

"We'd better get on with it," Rachel said. "Where are the instructions on simming it?"

"There aren't any. We have to explore the habitat, both in real time and virtually, and plan and build our colony while taking care of our bodily and mental requirements."

Rachel jammed her hands on her hips. "And whose stupid notion was that?" she drawled.

Harry shrugged and turned out his hands.

"Oh, really."

"It had to be that way. The current board can't micro-manage what they won't live to see. They can't know exactly what we'll face on the other side."

"I need to eat." She looked about the bland habitat. "How do we do that?" She stubbed her toe in the soil which looked all wrong to Harry.

"Initially, we'll subsist on ration packs to give us time to get crops started and to test native plants for compatibility."

"And the ration packs are — where?"

"I don't know."

"You helped plan this."

"Yes, theoretically, but I made sure I didn't know anything practical the rest of you wouldn't know."

Her lips shaped a comment she didn't voice.

He said, "I'm assuming they'd be somewhere in the ship."

31

"And where is the ship?"

Harry shrugged. "Let's go for a walk."

Rachel turned herself in a slow circle. "Out here isn't as big as it looks. It's mirrored. It's also not real. Nothing will grow here."

Harry took her word for it. Her hyper focus was something entirely rare. He'd heard of it—just—but it was an anomaly that couldn't be replicated, taught, or isolated. He wondered if it could be inherited or if it was an unstable mutation.

"It's also encapsulated," Rachel added. "There are other rooms like that one surrounding it." She pointed back through the French doors. "I think *they're* the ship. That one you were in is probably a hangar or storage space."

Again, Harry believed her.

"Can we get to the other rooms?" he asked.

"I expect so. They must all exit into *out there*. Mine did." She pointed to her left. "If we go out and walk the perimeter we should find ways in to all the rooms."

"Or others will find ways out."

"They won't have to. One-way windows. They'll be seeing what we saw, but from other angles. They'll come out."

"We'd better get started, then. But when we do find food, we'll have to eat cautiously."

"I already suck eggs."

"Ah. You're a nutritionist."

"I'm trained, but also an intuitive. I'll be able to tell you whether something is safe to eat by looking at it and smelling it." She must have seen his expression change. "Don't panic, Harry. I'll run the scientific tests as well, but they'll just confirm what I know already. It's pretty much impossible to poison me."

He grinned at her. "Very well, Doctor Traveller. In your considered opinion was that muck we consumed in the cubicles fit to eat?"

"No. It tried to be both inimical to bacteria *and* supportive of the human system. That's a bit of a contradiction."

"So you didn't drink it?"

"I did. Dying of thirst is a bad way to go, and I knew the sludge wouldn't kill me. I looked on it as a safer way of drinking bleach. By the way, I'm not a doctor."

"What is your official title then?"

"I don't have one. I could have been a doctor if I'd agreed to give up using clearsight. Only I couldn't do that. It's who I am."

Chapter Five: Sim, 2234

The sim was a bewildering mix of the real, the surreal, and the virtual.

The rooms were real, bland, and fairly featureless, but containing clues that could be spotted and interpreted via close attention and deduction.

The planet habitat *looked* real. It had trees, small plants, soil, and rock, but Harry thought it was sterile. Rachel concurred. She seemed unsure how she knew this, but it had to be her hyper focus.

The ration packs were concealed in an attic built into the seventh room they visited. By then, the company had increased to seventeen.

They were a mixed lot. Harry recognised some of them, but others weren't memorable or else were so changed by their gruelling decon treatment that they no longer resembled the subjects he'd seen at their interviews.

"Where are the others?" Abra Kiev asked. She was a tall woman with dark hair and an abrupt manner. She looked even gaunter than Rachel, as if nature had intended her to be Amazonian in build but had abandoned her halfway there. Harry wondered what had happened to make her look so starved. She might have been a runner, as he had designated so many applicants, but he suspected she was more like Flavia, using the meagre hand life dealt her with determination while not expecting joy.

She was the oldest of the elite, already past thirty-five.

Of course, she was being paid to live in the sim and to test the tanks. She was fit for that purpose, but Harry wondered whether she would be one who would cash out and opt to remain on Terra.

"There are supposed to be twenty of us," Paolo Paloma said. He was a biochemist, Harry recalled. He'd worn glasses during the interview, but he didn't have them now. His eyes looked a bit unfocused, but he must have good enough vision to manage without them — or else he'd had them corrected before entering the sim.

Harry hadn't been in charge of passing the applicants as physically fit, and without tests, he was unsure whether he would have passed Paloma or not.

Esme Crown was another person Harry recognised from the interviews, an ebullient woman of nineteen or so. She gave the impression of bouncing on the spot. He recalled that she was a physical training coach. She said, "Maybe the other three tapped out. Aborted the decon routine."

"I don't blame them," Genevieve Brant said with a shudder. "I thought about it, hard, but then I figured I'd be closing the door on shipping out."

"I thought of it too," a man Harry didn't know said. "Khanh Ho," he added, smiling about. "Does anyone have a personnel list so we can work out who's missing?"

They all shook their heads.

"Something else we'll have to find," Rachel said. "Or else we can just introduce ourselves. We have a year to do it. Whoever is missing can't really concern us."

Unless those people had essential skills and insights the rest of us lack, Harry thought.

Rachel indicated Room Seven. "Have any of you checked in there for food?"

"Are we supposed to?" Brant asked.

"There's no *supposed*. We're on a strange planet with the ship that brought us here. We've just woken to our new reality." Harry waved his hand at the room and Rachel quickly presented the theory that the rooms represented areas in the ship.

She stepped past Brant and scanned the walls, then opened two barely visible compartments. One held basic first aid equipment and the other, textbooks.

"Eureka!" she said a few minutes later. She pointed to a hatch set in the ceiling. "Ration packs."

"How do you know?" Ho asked, not challenging, but in seemingly honest curiosity.

"It seems likely," Rachel corrected herself. She didn't glance at Harry.

They spent some time looking for a ladder before concluding there wasn't one close by.

They were about to start stacking the wooden tables which would have meant unbolting them from the floor when Lolly Paringo, a tiny blonde woman with a perpetual smile, suggested a human pyramid.

She organised them so capably Harry wasn't surprised to learn she had been a performer with Cirque du Sud. Being the lightest of the elites, she scaled the pyramid and opened the hatch, hitched herself inside and bundled out a canvas bag of packs. It crunched. "Oops," Paringo said with a comical grimace. "Think I broke some crackers."

"Anything else up there?" Crown asked.

"Sure. Come up."

Crown scaled after her.

The pyramid unmade itself and the two above distributed various stores, lowering the heavier ones with ropes that were providentially stored with them.

Rachel cracked open a box of protein bars and took a careful bite. Her face screwed up with distaste, but she chewed and swallowed. "It's safe, nutritionally balanced, and rather revolting," she reported.

"I suppose we needn't worry about vermin in here," Ho

ventured, opening another box.

"Even if there were, they wouldn't eat this," Rachel muttered.

"There won't be any vermin in the ship," Harry said. "I'm not sure about the planet."

"It's not real, though," Steel Mercedes said.

"We have to act as if it is," Harry reminded. "And making the rations unpalatable is one way to ensure we eat to live and work hard to produce alternative food sources. On that point, are there any seeds up there?"

"Yes, all vacuum sealed," Crown called down. "Do we plant them right away?"

As the questions and speculations continued Harry felt a twinge of alarm. He had helped to select the elite adventurers — or at least, his reports had — but although those present were all undoubtedly intelligent, motivated, and physically gifted, their joint lack of method troubled him. He wondered if this bright influx of ideas would translate into the solid work needed to achieve results.

"Are there tree seeds?" he asked.

Crown dropped a pack of apple seeds into his hands. "I don't know why — we have a year in here and no fruit tree will bear much, if anything, in that time."

"That's that *act as if it's real*," Steel put in unexpectedly.

"So no counting down to sim-end and coasting," Abra Kiev said. "I tell my kids to work as hard at the end as at the beginning."

Harry glanced at her. "You have children?"

"Yes. Three. They're with my parents. I'm doing this for them."

Harry wondered if the board knew about those children, then recalled, again, that they were the viability team. That, he decided, was a better term for them than elites.

We should have had some solid worker ants — people who

can work without second-guessing, he thought, but then how many of that kind of person had applied? The board had chosen from those who saw the banner-ad, acted upon it, and passed the screening interviews, and who had not thought again or backed out before or during the decon. Intelligence and genetic excellence didn't necessarily translate to common sense.

He said, "We can't plant anything until we've tested the soil and growth conditions. We have to know what crops need which conditions and where to access the tools we'll need."

Lolly Paringo dropped out of the hatch and dangled from one hand. "There are tools here, and a crop-sim."

"A . . ."

"Crop-sim. It's the same as the acro-sim I used when I was in training for Cirque du Sud."

"Care to explain, Ms Paringo?" Harry asked.

"Call me Lolly. First names, eh?" She let go and dropped casually to land on her feet. She didn't even bend her knees. "Gather round, *mes enfants.*"

Everyone except Esme Crown did so. She lay on her stomach looking down through the hatch.

"An acro-sim is a light exoskeleton we 'bats use in training. It allows us to learn and practise feats without risking our limbs or sending insurance through the stratosphere. We climb in, so—" Lolly mimed stepping into boots and pulling a frame around her body. "We have sensors stuck, here and here . . . well, on whatever muscle groups we're training. Then we grab a trapeze or a spiral or rope or whatever and make the effort we think we'll need—" She reached up and executed a flexing spring. "The acro-sim sensors feed our effort back into the sim and the results come up on a screen. We don't attempt the real feat until we've scored green-to-go on at least twenty consecutive attempts."

"Can that translate to non-acrobatic feats?" Rachel asked.

"It can be used to learn sports skills, driving, swimming, horse-riding, and so on. Just input what you're trying to achieve, and the acro tells you if you can do it or if you would have failed and been injured. The crop-sim up there is the same idea, but it works in the virtual world. So, you put in the effort of, say, hoeing or digging, and it translates that to virtual weeding or planting. Get it?"

"How does that grow us food?" Kiev asked.

Lolly shrugged her shoulders to her ears. "I don't know."

Harry said, "I'd guess whatever we grow through our physical efforts in the virtual world will be grown in the physical world outside the sim and delivered to us through a one-way hatch."

"Makes sense," Lolly said. "Same with animals. I'm betting there are agri-sims and all sorts. I don't expect they have real animals in here. That'd need a proper eco-system."

Lolly proved correct. By the end of the first two weeks in the sim, the viabilities had found a great many hidden sims, including an exploration module that allowed them to explore in a virtual Magellan Sixteen.

It was harder work than any of them expected or were used to, and they had to put in long hours of physical effort. The temperature inside the habitat changed, and light mimicked the progression of days. Rain and wind alternated with sunlight.

After the nothingness of the decon cubicles, it was a relief to get their rhythms back.

The ration packs, which no one ate for fun, lasted until the first of their virtual crops matured. After that, they ate sporadically of tatsoi, baby beets, radish, lettuce, arugula and other greens that appeared in the habitat. Finger carrots came next, then cucumbers.

Protein was more difficult to earn, but milk and cheese came from the virtual goats, and eggs from the virtual ducks.

The work, though hard and repetitive, lacked the smells and dirt of true agricultural labour, but they soon became used to the rotation of jobs. A treadmill allowed them to climb virtual hills and their hands became calloused from friction with real manual tools.

"If we don't work, we don't eat," as Abra put it. She and Steel Mercedes, the metallurgist, had paired up to build an actual dwelling on the planet, using found materials from crates and hatches. They had laid out a virtual village and marked up the foundations for a dairy and shearing shed.

Shearing the virtual long-haired goats resulted in blisters for the shearers and a delivery of actual raw fleeces, which Ho spun using a hand spindle and which he and Harry knitted up into blankets which were welcome as the artificial weather cooled.

Lacking the materials for a loom, they chose a virtual tree and spent many sweaty hours chopping, trimming, and sawing, leaving it to cure in the virtual sun. They made pegs using nails from the supply and experimented with different weights of yarn.

In between subsistence work, which took up much of the day, there was study, done the old-fashioned way from books with no feedback.

After noting the poor performance of this method, Harry organised classes in anything and everything any of them could teach.

He and Esme Crown dealt with the minor injuries resulting from the work, and Crown and Lolly Paringo taught the others remedial massage for the frequent headaches they all experienced.

"What *is* causing this?" Rachel asked, rubbing her temples.

"Eyestrain from books," Paolo said.

She shook her head, wincing. "It's not that. Might be lack of some trace nutrients. The soil here isn't optimum. Maybe we were meant to augment it somehow. Composting would be the obvious way, but—"

"Chicken and egg," Abra put in. "We need excess vegetation to make compost, and the crops so far are low waste."

"I think it's the air," Field Shaloman said quietly. He was a midwife, whose work skills seemed unlikely to be needed in the sim, though they would be useful for the eventual colony.

Rachel squinted at him. "I hope not."

"It's as good a theory as any," Harry said.

"But that means there's nothing we can do about it. The air's so filtered it's as flat as boiled water. We can't put in the normal impurities the way we can bolster the soils with organic matter and minerals—once we get enough of it." She groaned. "Hasn't anyone any ideas?"

Harry looked her over. Everyone except the programmer Williams Williams appeared sallow, and even Williams' black skin was duller than it should be. He was another whose skills, which lay in the gaming industry, seemed an unlikely choice for the sim. However, he was skilled at spinning scenarios from facts and supposition.

Rachel's olive skin also seemed dull, and Harry saw pain in her eyes. He suspected she might have tapped out if it had been an option.

It wasn't. It had been made clear that the sim would run for the scheduled year and there would be no outside intervention even if someone had a catastrophic accident or was murdered. They were to deal with anything that happened exactly as if they were centuries from home. He had no doubt they were being monitored, but nothing was ever delivered in the *drops* that they hadn't produced virtually for themselves. He wondered if there were medicinal herb seeds anywhere on the ship. Lolly and Esme had not reported any.

"I know something that might help," he said half reluctantly. Like Rachel with her hyper focus, he had elected not to share all his talents with others in the group. He knew Rachel was nervous about being regarded as a freak or being asked to teach what she could not. His reticence was more to do with not wanting the others to be suspicious of what he might be able to do to them. As far as he could tell, only Rachel knew or even suspected he had been part of the team who chose them.

He thought it healthy to keep some secrets. That allowed everyone to hold on to the illusion of choice.

"Let's have it, Harry," Paloma said. He raised his hand to his face, then lowered it again. Harry perceived he was mentally polishing his vanished glasses. His eyes seemed not-quite focused.

He hadn't had them corrected, Harry decided. He probably intended to do that with the payment from the sim.

He wondered if he was the only one who had parlayed the holding payment into immediately accessible funds. Probably not. These were clever people. He expected Abra at least would have engineered some payment for her children.

"How many of you can put yourselves into a trance?" he asked.

"What, like self-hypnosis?" Williams seemed interested rather than threatened.

"You could call it that. A light trance makes time seem to speed up, and you can watch your own personal movie, listen to music, or look out over the ocean—even spend time with someone you know outside, though that's probably not a good idea. Time out might help with the headaches. Think of it as sending your minds and bodies on a little holiday somewhere peaceful."

"What, like the virtual exploration?" Williams sounded doubtful now. The sim had decided he'd gone too far from the ship one day and made him sleep out overnight.

"No, that's generated by the sim. You generate your trance experiences yourselves. It's not meditation. You're not blanking your thoughts. You're making a scene to calm and entertain your mind."

The others exchanged speculative glances.

"I'll have a shot at it," Lolly said. "It doesn't sound too different from putting myself in the zone, and I've been doing that all my working life." She glanced at Esme. "I suppose you do it too."

"Mm."

"Do you want to try it, Rachel?" Harry asked.

She nodded painfully. "If you think it will help."

"I think it *might*," he said cautiously. It had occurred to him that Rachel's hyper focus might be the reason her headaches were worse than the others'. She might never switch off.

The first session was difficult. The viability team members were all used to having their minds busy. Coaxing them to relax went against their natural inclinations.

Harry gave up on using the same visualisations for all of them, and instead offered one-on-one sessions as a shortcut to finding out what worked for each.

He met with varying success, but to his surprise, Rachel proved easy to hypnotise. He hadn't tried that with any of the others, out of caution. Who knew how they might react if they knew what he could do?

With Rachel, he took the risk. He watched the pain lines fade from her face and patiently offered her different scenes, from a walk through a rose garden to flickering candlelight and birdsong. The one that worked best was a misty night sky with stars occasionally showing through the clouds of vapor.

He sat with her, holding her hand and listening to the others conversing quietly as they compared their own self-generated mind-journeys.

After thirty minutes, he squeezed her hand. "Rachel."

She lay unmoving.

"Rachel."

"What is it?" Field Shaloman, maybe alerted by the tone of his voice, had come up beside him. He looked down. "That doesn't look like a light trance to me, Harry."

It didn't look like one to Harry, either.

"I'm always aware of voices if someone speaks to me while I'm under," Field said.

"Rachel," Harry said.

Genevieve Brant tiptoed over. "You'd better kiss her, Harry. That's the traditional way to wake a sleeping beauty."

"Or just let her come out of it when she's ready," Shaloman said. "She must be your best student."

Harry was pondering that when Rachel abruptly opened her eyes.

She sat up. "What are you all staring at?"

"Nothing at all," Genevieve said airily. "How do you feel?"

"Fine." Rachel wriggled her shoulders. "Quite fine. Really well." She smiled at Harry. "Did you see that silvery mist?"

"No." He willed her not to suggest it had been a shared experience.

"Neither did I. I just saw the night with a few stars and nothing going on. It was *brilliant.*" She reached out and grabbed Harry by the arms. "My hero. You gave me the gift of emptiness."

"Surely, you gave it to yourself," Field said mildly.

He glanced at Harry and gave a tiny nod.

Field *knew.* He was not about to mention it.

"Are you really feeling better?" Harry asked when the others had dispersed.

Rachel beckoned him closer. "I will be when I've had my kiss."

Chapter Six: Extraction, 2234-35

The virtual seasons turned, and Harry started to feel as if he'd always been in the sim and always would be.

Sometimes he focused on memories of his childhood, his training, or his last visit with Flavia and Harley. They seemed far away. He remembered scenes and sounds, conversations and feelings, but none of it felt real. It was like hearing a story recited in a flat monotone, with everything present except the colours of emotion.

Despite his early misgivings, the viability team proved an excellent blend of aptitude and personality. Perhaps because they were all elite and capable, none seemed to feel it necessary to prove it. Williams even ventured that it was a relief to be able to converse without having to explain himself.

There was no leader.

Everyone worked because, as Abra put it, *no work, no eat.*

Crucially, no one seemed to be fretting for their former lives. Harry thought they probably all felt distanced, the way he did. They had all tied things up, relinquishing living quarters and resigning from former positions. As far as he knew, only Abra had young children. Martin Fong, the mechanical inventor, had a child, but that, he'd explained, had been by arrangement for a couple who wanted to raise it without his input.

Harry was careful to keep these ponderings to himself unless someone asked. His role as counsellor and psych observer was supposed to have terminated as soon as he entered the sim. He was not obliged to observe or to report on his companions.

And of course, there was Rachel. The way he felt about Rachel perplexed him. He'd had girlfriends, when his studies and work permitted him the time, and he'd sometimes contemplated becoming a family man.

His parents hadn't been copybook examples, but he wasn't them. He had become fond of Harley and had seen how having a child added purpose to Flavia's life.

Before that, he wanted a companion—someone who understood life the way he did, who would love him for himself and not from some obligation or custom. Ideally, his companion would be independent and accepting.

Rachel was that companion in the sim, but she was not the sort of woman who generally attracted him. His previous girlfriends had been cool intellectuals, precise, curvy—and blonde. Rachel was fervent, lean, and olive-skinned.

That was why he felt perplexed.

The viabilities hadn't been forbidden from forming relationships in the sim. The purpose of their year was to test how people with no previous knowledge of one another would form a working community when they had no outside influences or avenues of escape. Nothing was forbidden, other than taking anything into the sim, which would have been impossible anyway. No one had bothered with body cavity searches. The sludge and laxative water would have rendered that impractical.

Harry's professional self watched the developing social connections with interest. Abra Kiev and Steel Mercedes were sleeping together in the cottage they'd made. Lolly and Esme had formed a close friendship that seemed in no way romantic. They were the youngest, so they were probably natural companions. They were both energetic and flexible and surprisingly strong, but they never seemed in competition. Harry saw them comparing and trading skills.

Genevieve Brant, an architect, and Til Lund, a quiet historian, always chose to work together, while Field the midwife,
the geologist Sofia Kataranga, and the veterinarian Jonty Lane
made an oddly compatible polyamorous trio.

Harry wondered how and whether these relationships
would continue when they left the sim, and what would happen if one of them resulted in a child.

"Not going to happen," Sofia told him as they worked the
pump to water the greens.

"Implant?"

"Obviously. Jonty and me and Gen, anyway—we've all got
sevens, and I'm betting the others have too. Don't want things
getting too realistic, do we? Of course, we didn't know Field
would be along to catch any little oopsies. The poor dear is
going to be *so* rusty when we get out."

Harry supposed he should have known all that.

For all his interested observation of the couples and
groups, he found he couldn't apply his scientific gaze to the
dynamic between himself and Rachel. It was too unknowable
and too close to home.

"Where do you see us this time next year?" he asked her.

They'd climbed into the storage hatch in Room Seven, using the rope ladder they'd made and which they'd pulled up
behind them. It was the only place they could depend on being undisturbed.

Rachel lifted her head from his shoulder. "Well, we won't
be here."

"Obviously not."

"Unless they forget we're in the sim and leave us here."

He laughed.

"You're right. They won't do that while they have to keep
feeding us. If they *have* to keep feeding us."

"What do you mean?"

Rachel poked him in the ribs. "I mean, maybe we're really

in tanks and halfway to Magellan Sixteen and this virtual life is really a virtual version of a virtual tank-dream."

That was so surreal he didn't laugh it off.

"What if we are?" Rachel said dreamily. "We might wake up one morning and find we're doing all this for real. It wouldn't matter. We all had to wind up our lives before we came to the sim. We've nowhere else to be."

"I wouldn't mind," Harry said. He thought of Flavia and Harley, but they seemed like vague watercolours fading on a wall.

Hope you're enjoying unlimited cheese, Turq.

"Neither would I," Rachel said. "I won't mind anything, really, as long as we're together."

"You see us together in a year?"

"Don't you?"

He realised he did. However he looked at his future, Rachel was there. "In more than a year. In a decade. When we ship out for real, we can go as a family with our kids."

"You want kids?"

"Yes. We'll have to get cracking before we ship out," he said, remembering Flavia's bleak mention of her age. "Marry me, Rach?"

"Try and stop me! But not in here. This is a sim. I want it to be real." She poked his ribs again. "Can you sort out my head so I can feel well enough to sort you out?"

"Yes. Rach—"

"Hmm?"

"Did you get these headaches before you came into the sim? Honestly, now."

She sat up abruptly. "Of course not! I've always been the picture of health. They'd never have let me in otherwise!"

"If they knew."

"There was nothing *to* know."

"Okay," he soothed her. "Let's have a trip to the misty sky. Ready?"

"Oh, my emptiness," she murmured.

Harry ran through the simple routine that put Rachel into her trance. She was the most suggestible subject he'd ever had, which was odd. There was nothing suggestible about her otherwise.

They kept a log of their time in the sim. By the time the year drew to its close, there was a mass of written material documenting work done, crops raised, innovations, achievements, and even personal assessments. The log also held a large list of items they thought should have been supplied.

Chief among these were herb seeds and far more raw materials such as paper, ready-made panels, more tools, and better texts for animal husbandry. They wanted genetic codes as well, and a better balance of skills and specialisations. They had muddled through for a year, but seventeen adults without dependent children or frail elders in a safe environment could afford to spend more time learning and failing than settlers on a real extra-sol planet would be able to have.

"Backups and fail-safes," as Williams put it. "They'll need duplicates of duplicates of tools and knowledge bases."

"We made a start on that," Genevieve pointed out. "Harry's training sessions mean we could all sub for at least one or two of the others at a pinch. Intellectually speaking, of course. I can't lift Williams above my head, but he could lift me."

"And when we ship out there will be far more of us, with more skills and plenty of duplication," Field said. "I could train midwives, but some disciplines need special talents that can't be taught."

None of them knew exactly when the sim would end, and besides, they'd agreed with Abra that they needed to work right to the end, as if their situation was permanent.

By Harry's calculations they'd been in the sim for three

hundred and ninety-seven days. That was more than a year, but the only way they had to count the days was by the alternation of light and dark. It seemed likely that someone had decreed the "days" should be a different length, mimicking the rotation of Magellan Sixteen.

Some of the others disagreed, suggesting the nights were shorter and the days longer.

Without working timepieces, no one knew.

Lolly's suggestion of counting seconds from daybreak to dark wasn't a serious one, and Genevieve's sketch for a sundial never got any further, because, as she admitted, the "sun" was artificial anyway.

"Someone should have had a baby," Field said, straight-faced. "If it was planted the day we got here—"

Rachel threw a cabbage leaf at him. "Speak for yourself! None of us was in any shape for planting *anything*. The poor kid would have starved in utero after what that poison sludge did to our systems."

They were noisily arguing the point amid a hail of the peanuts someone had managed to grow from the ration packs when a loud klaxon brought them to attention.

They froze. It was the first sound they hadn't made themselves.

Then a voice said briskly, "Good afternoon, elite adventurers. Please return to the decon cubicles you occupied initially for extraction. Take nothing with you. You have ten minutes, starting *now*."

Another voice, clearly mechanical, started the countdown, too loudly for any conversation.

Rachel grabbed Harry's hand, but when they attempted to enter the same cubicle it flashed a red light. Letters chased themselves across the door. *Oneonlyoneonlyoneonly . . .*

"I'll see you at the debriefing," Harry yelled. He kissed Rachel and saw her into the cubicle before heading for his own.

They had never returned to these during the sim because the doors had locked as they left. He hoped there would be no decon to endure.

There would be no point. The sim had no bacteria not already present outside.

To his relief, the board must have come to the same conclusion. He was ordered to strip and shower and asked to dress himself in the clothing he had worn before he entered the cubicle over a year ago.

He recognised the clothing. It had evidently been laundered, but the fit was poor. He concluded he'd lost fat and gained muscle.

He hoped to meet Rachel on the other side, but as he stepped out of the cubicle he felt a tiny prick in his shoulder muscle. He turned angrily and —

Chapter Seven: What's Today? 2235

Harry woke wearing a hospital gown, lying on a chilly bed and hooked up to various beeping equipment.

"Oh, would you then?" he enquired with as much sarcasm as he could muster.

He sat up and methodically unclipped, unhooked and un-plumbed himself.

He left the pulse monitor until last and was unsurprised when it shrieked a protest as he disconnected it.

Rapid footsteps approached and two medics in blue gowns, caps, and masks burst in to find Harry, not flatlining, but sitting on the bed swinging his bare legs.

"Good afternoon. Unless it's morning. What's today?" he asked.

It was odd to see someone other than the sixteen other via-bilities, but he was too much of an old hand to let that show.

"Tuesday." The taller one sounded nonplussed.

"Date?"

"January the tenth."

Harry sighed. "Year?"

"Twenty-two thirty-six."

So—it *had* been more than a year. He wondered if he should check the fine print and make a fuss, but what was the point? He belonged to Outward Bound.

"What hospital is this?"

They didn't answer. Neither did they approach to check his vitals manually.

"Fair enough. I need a release form to sign. Or someone to

debrief me." He clicked his fingers. "*Vite, vite!*"

He didn't see or hear the signal, but there must have been one, because someone came unhurriedly into the room. This person wasn't gowned or masked, but she wore a clear face-plate respirator.

"I'm not infectious," Harry said waspishly.

"I'm aware of that, Doctor Fejoa," the woman said.

"Then why the haz-per?"

She lifted a gloved hand to touch the plate. "This is for your protection, not mine."

"*You're* infectious?"

"No. But you have spent an extended time away from the normal pathogens. You will be vulnerable to infection and to adverse reactions from irritants. Therefore, you will be quarantined and monitored for a period of thirty days."

Harry tried to remember if he'd known this beforehand. He supposed it could be taken as tacitly agreed because it was logical.

"What happens after that?"

"You will be gradually exposed to semi-filtered air and monitored for —"

Harry held up his hand. "That can't be done here."

"This is a sterile environment."

"I know, but it's not good for our mental, physical and emotional health to be shut away in a hospital setting. We've all worked damned hard for over a year as guinea pigs. It's well known that *any* exercise regimen has to be tapered, not brought to an abrupt halt. We — my fellow viabilities and I — require a gradual tapering back to normal service. That means an opportunity to exercise and to debrief among ourselves."

The woman looked pensive. "That's not in our instructions."

"It is now. Fix it."

"I'll see what can be managed," the woman said.

"Don't do that. Fix it. And if you don't have the authority to fix it, send me someone who does." Having tossed his dice again, Harry risked one more small touch. "By the way, do not anesthetise me, or any of us, again without warning and our written and informed permission. It's unethical and unnecessary. We are paid volunteers, and if we feel coerced or ill-treated, the results of the tests we're undertaking will be compromised. What's your name?"

The woman touched her name tag.

"Come closer. I have normal vision, but you're too far away for me to read that."

She stood her ground.

Harry nodded. "You can't, can you? You're on the other side of a barrier. That face plate is just for show. You'll have to tell me."

"I am Doctor Swan."

"Helene Swan?"

She inclined her head.

"Thank you. Let me know when the arrangements are made. And in the meantime, I need to see Rachel Traveller."

"Isolation is —"

"Unnecessary in our case. We've been together for a year in the same habitat."

Swan nodded to the two gowned medics. "Bring Traveller."

She left.

Harry blew out his cheeks. He hoped his performance had been convincing. The object of the sim, quite apart from testing the effect of an unfamiliar work regime and no contact with the outside world, was undoubtedly to monitor the effect on personality. He had been dictatorial when he demanded the release of funds and again when he forced transparency in the matter of Chavez' *tacit agreement*. He trusted his latest strop would prove that the waspish Harry Fejoa was intact.

He was still thinking about that when a figure in a full-body suit and respirator stumbled through an airlock.

He felt a ridiculous smile break over his face.

"Rach!"

He slid down from his perch on the bed and hurried to embrace her, changed his mind and helped her to unclip the suit.

Clad in a blue hospital gown like his, she looked both vulnerable and adorable.

He said, without preamble, "They're letting us out into a zoo."

"With or without animals?" she asked, hugging him.

"Darling Rach, we *are* the animals."

Their zoo was a disused island motel. It was somewhat run down, but it had real grounds, a real beach, cliffs, and comfortably appointed rooms that had been mothballed sixty years before.

They travelled by boat in full-body suits, but as soon as they were decanted and the crew had left, Lolly Paringo shucked hers off and flung herself at Harry.

"You're a star! I was ready to murder someone!"

Harry considered saying it was nothing to do with him but elected to go with a version of the truth. "I just gave them my professional opinion. They want us in optimum shape for the tanking tests, and keeping us trapped in sterile rooms isn't the way to that destination."

"What happens now?" Abra Kiev dropped her suit on the sand and gave it a sly kick.

Harry waited until they were all unsuited, revealing clothing similar to what they'd worn in the sim. "I don't know, exactly. I suspect we'll be monitored from a distance, but otherwise let alone to reacclimatise to normal conditions. It won't be too difficult, because there's no industrialisation here now."

Rachel, who had been tucked under his arm after Lolly retreated from her hug, stepped away and stretched, inhaling salty air. "This is *so* much better than the sim. The colours are real, and so is the breeze."

Harry said, "They might have a point about allergies and sensitivities. If anyone has any symptoms, don't be a hero. We have basic first aid in the stores."

"But none of us has allergies," Williams pointed out. "We'd never have made the cut if we had."

"It's possible to acquire them. And for now, we'd better get these food stocks into the building."

Field said, "It's as well we built some muscles in the sim."

The mothballed motel proved an ideal setting to wind down. The electronics were decommissioned, but there was enough printed material for them to piece together its history. Brierly Island had been a holiday destination when such things still existed, but successive recessions, labour laws, and fuel shortages had seen it closed down in 2175. Harry didn't know how or why it had been selected for their reintegration. He suspected one of the board-members had family connections to the original owners.

The unknown schedule of the tank tests lay ahead, but none of the viabilities discussed it openly. Neither did they discuss the way they saw their future or whether they planned to ship out eventually—at least not with Harry. It was enough that they were out of the sim and one step closer to whatever came next.

The first they knew of that next step of their journey was when the boat that had brought them to the island returned. A single figure disembarked and walked up the steps towards the motel.

"That's Chavez," Rachel said.

Harry didn't ask her how she knew.

"I expect he's come for the debriefing," he said. "Let's go and meet him."

Hand-in-hand, they walked to the top of the steps.

Chavez inspected them with slightly scornful eyes. "Well, Doctor Fejoa. A year in the sim didn't sweeten your disposition."

"Did you expect it to?" Harry asked.

The man shrugged. "I didn't expect my chief medic to resign. Let's walk along the cliffs. We need to talk."

"Is this the official debriefing?" Harry asked.

"No. It's an informal conversation."

"Fine," Harry said. "Coming Rach?"

"Just you."

"No. Rachel and I are together. We're planning to marry. She's welcome to hear anything you have to say to me."

Chavez gave him a hard stare, then nodded. "If you insist. Have you told her you work for us?"

"We all work for you."

"In your professional capacity, during the initial interviews, passing psychological assessments."

"I knew about that," Rachel said. She added, "And it's just as well. Some personality types wouldn't have been able to deal with the sim."

Chavez grunted. "Come on, then."

They walked away from the buildings and out along the rocks. Harry waited for whatever the man had in mind.

Finally Chavez said, abruptly, "In your opinion, how did the sim perform?"

"It was artificial," Harry said.

"Obviously. We couldn't send you to a planet."

Rachel said, "You could have sent us here, though. We'd have been cut off from the outside, and we could have grown real crops and had real animals. It would have been more realistic."

Chavez grunted again. "You misunderstood the question. The sim was, as you say, artificial, though the work you performed required real effort. How did the elites perform within the sim?"

Harry said, "Surprisingly well. There were enough of us that the isolation wasn't a problem."

"Mentally and emotionally?"

"Much better than I would have expected, but then you chose self-sufficient candidates."

"Some of the board seemed to think homesickness would be a problem—that being cut off from normal routine would send some subjects into depressive states or cause conflict over petty jealousies. There was also concern that being away from news and societal issues would have caused mental inertia from the lack of context and stimulation."

"None of that happened."

"We were too tired to be homesick, and too busy to miss the news," Rachel said. "And it was artificial."

"So you said." Chavez sounded annoyed.

"Too artificial to be immersive."

Chavez' face pinched. "As I just explained—"

Rachel cut him off. "Mister Chavez, I'm talking about our knowledge that we were in there for a finite period. That's what's artificial. We knew we would be coming out and broadly, when, so there was no long-term investment in the place. An open-ended community on this island would have given a much better result."

Still looking angry, Chavez said, "You're speaking for yourself?"

"Yes." Rachel sounded puzzled.

"Doctor Fejoa hasn't coached you?"

"I don't understand the question."

Harry said blandly, "That would have been counterproductive, Chavez. It could also have compromised Rachel's safety. We worked together in reasonable harmony because, as Rachel says, we knew it was finite, we were all there by our own will, and we were too damned tired to plot revolution. Nevertheless, each of us had our own personal experience. You will note that in the personal logs. I have no idea what anyone else wrote in these. For all I know there could be outpourings of angst and dislike."

"I see." Chavez stopped walking. "Come then, it's time to return to the Outward Bound facility for the next round of interviews and debriefing. And this time, you will *not* know what to expect."

Chapter Eight: Debriefed, 2235

The debriefing, when it finally happened, was a protracted affair.

It included medical examinations, mechanical tests such as weighing, measuring, and calculating levels of fat, muscle, bone density, calcium, and serotonin. They were put through fitness tests and given cognitive and general knowledge tests and an odd written examination that included questions requiring specialised knowledge not all of them could be expected to have.

Harry found no trouble with most of the questions. What he hadn't known already he'd picked up from the lecture sessions they'd held in the sim.

Some questions were impenetrable, though. Harry had heard of string theory, cross-stitch, and tropical fish, but he couldn't answer the questions pertaining to these. He had a good memory and an organised mind, but he could not recall what he'd never known.

During a long test that consisted of sitting still and identifying sounds on the edge of audibility, he put a question to Cataleya Conti. She sat placidly embroidering in an armchair, looking like everyone's least memorable aunt. The sight of her needle making precise movements reminded him of the cross-stitch question in the exam.

"What was the purpose of that odd exam?" he asked.

"Listen for the sounds," she reproved.

Harry removed his headphones.

Conti, with a tiny frown for his recalcitrance, touched a

button on the panel beside her. "I'm pausing the program."

"Good."

"Tell me when you feel like cooperating," she added politely.

Harry wondered what it would take to make her express anger. Now was probably not a good time to ask. "What was the —"

"You know that already," she cut in.

Harry thought he probably did. "Choosing the viabilities from a wide range of disciplines was deliberate."

"Obviously, a wide selection of aptitudes is needed for successful colonisation," Conti said. She added, in a pensive tone, "History has taught us about the need for multiple facets. Take the nineteenth century explorers. They had bravery, determination, curiosity —"

"But no common sense," Harry supplied.

"Quite so. They showed a mathematical inability to divide a journey by the number of days, the number of miles, the terrain, and their portable supplies. Factor in the unlikelihood of finding free water in a dry continent and —" She shrugged.

"There are lots of randoms in that equation."

"True, but if you take the basics — food for one man and one horse for one day's travel, multiply by the number of men and horses in a party — now halve that number and you have the maximum number of days for safe travel. Reach that number and, unless more food is immediately available, you turn around. If you don't, you are too optimistic for your own good. It's not a survival trait."

"The colonists won't be able to turn back."

"No. Hence the need for as many options otherwise — and a much wider range of personalities."

Harry said, "You wanted to see if we'd learn from one another and make practical decisions?"

She inclined her head.

"And maybe you wanted to know *what* we'd learn that didn't have an immediate practical application."

Conti pulled her needle through the fabric and made a neat knot. "Obviously. There's more to a successful society than practical application."

"You need brain furniture. It *was* pretty obvious. What are the conclusions?"

She shrugged. "I don't know. Teams of behaviouralists and educators are collating that information."

"You're not one of them?"

"No. I'm a nursery teacher when I'm not working here."

I wonder why that doesn't surprise me, Harry thought.

"Think about it," he said, briskly stuffing the conversational boots with *her* feet.

Conti shrugged again. "I'm supposing it's been noted that some skills and knowledge can be transferred and shared, and some can't. Skill versus talent. Synaesthesia cannot be taught. Neither can musicality or even common sense. Everyone knows that."

Field had said as much, so Harry thought Conti was right. "The questions were to see what, if anything, we'd learned about the aptitudes and disciplines of one another, but—" He broke off.

"What's wrong?" Conti asked. Her smooth forehead creased in a blink-and-he'd-miss-it frown.

Harry lifted a hand and gave himself a light thump on the head. "Getting sluggish here. The questions most of us wouldn't be able to answer were to do with aptitudes the three others had. The ones who aborted the decon."

"Were they?" She rethreaded her needle and made a precise stitch. He wondered what she was making. From the angle of his seat he couldn't see enough to tell.

Rachel could. The thought lifted his heart on a bubble of joy. His Rachel saw more than most, but she'd still cast her lot in with him.

"Or else they were randomly generated and there never were three other people," he added. He waited a beat. "I suppose you could have answered the question about the earliest known example of cross-stitch."

"It was found in a Coptic tomb in Egypt, dating from the sixth century AD," she said.

Harry put his headphones back on.

Mind games.

He played them himself sometimes. Conti was good at them—much better than Chavez, because she was likeable.

He lifted one earpiece away from his head. "What do you call your spaniel, Ms Conti?"

"Picasso."

"How many spaniels have you had?"

"This is the fifth, if you count the family pet when I was a teenager."

"What did you call the first one of your own?"

She favoured him with a faint smile. "Picasso." She added thoughtfully, "I'm a creature of habit."

Harry smiled ruefully back. He remembered his once-upon-a-time desire to take Cataleya Conti to dinner and to find out what made her tick. That was before Rachel. He'd never do it now.

Pity.

Then, of course, he wondered *why* he'd never do it now. He'd never been interested in Conti romantically, and she certainly wasn't interested in him.

It just felt somehow inappropriate.

How very odd.

Eventually, the multi-faceted debriefing ended.

After that came what Harry thought of as an audience with the board. There were a dozen members, including Conti,

Ash, Woo, Chavez, and the seventeen viabilities.

After general conversation and an official thank you to all participants, Chavez, the usual mouthpiece, said, "The simulation experiment was a modest success. We have collected a great deal of data and our knowledge of how isolation affects the human psyche is somewhat advanced. However, we have concluded that our choice of candidates was too narrow."

Chavez paused, and Rachel nudged Harry. "I thought—" She broke off.

Harry put his arm around her. He had an inkling of what Chavez was about to say.

"The range of specialisations was broad, ranging from the purely physical"—his gaze touched on Lolly Paringo, who looked instantly annoyed—"to the highly intellectual"—he glanced at Khanh Ho—"to the practical. However, in choosing participants who are elite in their fields, we failed to provide for a good mix of temperaments and resilience.

"In short"—his cold gaze roamed the audience—"we made no provision for normal human nature. The elites have no concept of failure and no sense of inferiority. They performed the tasks necessary and added more content to the sim, yet the effect was not so much that of a quasi-colony as it was a personal challenge and elite bonding exercise. They learned nothing from the experience. They failed to grow."

Harry glanced around at the faces of people he'd come to regard as friendly acquaintances if not as close friends. Rachel huffed a tiny laugh.

"What's biting you?" Harry whispered.

"Could he have been more offensive?"

"Possibly, but that would have been over-egging the pudding."

"I thought Lolly was going to throw something at him."

"She might have if she'd thought there was a shred of justice in what he said."

"But there was," Rachel said.

Harry gave her a one-armed hug. "I know. That's what makes him so dangerous. That mix of chill truth and wicked oversimplification. Lolly's physicality is impressive, but she's got a sharp intellect, and Ho might know his way around atomic particles but he's as practical as any. Chavez was right about one thing, though—"

"The failure bit?"

"Yes. If it hadn't been *safe* in there and if we hadn't had the timeline, or if our efforts hadn't translated into successful harvests, then it might have been a far nastier experience. If we hadn't worked we could have starved, but none of us was ever going to behave in a self-destructive way. We're too—"

"Intelligent," Rachel said.

"Programmed, I was going to say. We are domesticated. We are probably too satisfied with ourselves. We wanted to gain something from the experience, but we thought of that in terms of advancing our chances, not ourselves."

Chavez had moved back, and Bindilina Ash, a cheery-looking redhead, took his place.

"The debriefing is done, and you have all been deemed at least as healthy—and in some cases more so—as you were when you came into the program," she said. "At this point, we'll move to the tank tests on schedule. Therefore, we're calling for volunteers for the first of these tests."

Abra Kiev said, "What if we don't volunteer?"

"Then you'll be paid for your input so far and released from the project as originally agreed. That was made clear to you when you signed your contract."

"I thought the parameters might have changed while we were out of the loop," Abra said shortly.

"That would have been unethical."

Abra's expression suggested she didn't find that an impediment. Harry, recalling the funds in the holding account, didn't blame her. He believed the board would hold to the letter of the contracts they had signed, but he also knew most contracts could be open to interpretation. Any contract containing the words *circumstances beyond our control* was as watertight as a sieve.

Williams half raised his hand. "If we elect to leave for a while then come back for the second or third round of tank tests, is that acceptable?"

"No," Chavez said. "That would amount to trying to claim a benefit you hadn't earned."

Abra nodded as if this agreed with her initial understanding. "And if we don't volunteer we lose our preferred status for shipping out."

"Provisionally," Ash said. "You could reapply if you chose—not for the tanking, but for the colony. That will be an ongoing process for some years to come."

"Then I'll be leaving, thanks," Abra said. "Who do I see about cashing out?"

"That would be me," Bao Woo said with a tiny bow. "If you come with me, we'll sign the releases and transfer the funds to your nominated account with immediate availability." He glanced at Harry, who nodded back.

Abra looked around at the others. "This is probably goodbye, but I wish you all the best of luck. Maybe we'll meet again on Magellan Sixteen." She made her way over to Woo.

Steel Mercedes shot a rueful grin around the room. "Entreat me not to leave thee," he said and followed.

Paolo Paloma hesitated and went after them.

Harry saw Genevieve Brant make a hesitant step then glance first at Esme and Lolly then at Til Lund. He smiled and half beckoned. Brant gave a tiny shrug and walked over to stand beside him.

"Anyone else?" Bindilina Ash asked in a cheerful voice. She might have been offering them another cup of tea.

Genevieve said, "Can we go to the tank briefing before we make up our minds? I want the details so I can make an informed decision on the risks."

Chavez scowled but Ash said calmly, "That will be fine, obviously. None of us wants you to feel pressured or to miss out on the great adventure from needless apprehension."

"I'll stay then. I've come this far —"

"Exactly," Ash said, still smiling. "We'll hand you over to Doctor Dash Darling who can answer your questions."

Harry heard Rachel give her little huff of a laugh at the name before they both turned to see who owned it.

DDD, as Rachel irreverently termed him later, was tall and ungainly with disturbingly light grey eyes.

He stepped out from among the board members and beckoned to the fourteen remaining viabilities.

"Come this way."

They followed silently, stepping out through an opaque door in his wake.

Harry glanced sideways in case anyone was armed with an anaesthetic gun, but it appeared his words — or maybe common sense — had come into play. Instead of being knocked out, they were invited into the back of a large vehicle. It looked comfortably appointed and it would have held the entire seventeen if they had all elected to come.

"One-way windows," Rachel said aloud.

"As in we can see out, but others can't see in?" Cherry York asked hopefully.

"The other way around."

Genevieve balked. "I've changed my mind."

"I have too," Tyler Low, the cinematographer, said. "I've had enough of being led about with a hood over my eyes."

"Hoodwinked," Cherry said.

"Verily," Low agreed cordially. He stepped over to Cherry and kissed her. "Chez moi, it's been a pleasure."

"Oh, it has." She patted his cheek, hesitated, and moved towards the truck.

"And then there were twelve," Rachel stated, deadpan.

She and Harry climbed into the truck in Cherry's wake, followed by Martin Fong, the eldest of them now Abra had left, and the others, leaving Low and Brant standing together and looking a little defiant and quite a bit lost.

Til Lund paused and looked back.

Genevieve Brant met his gaze then turned away.

Lund got into the truck.

Harry did a quick head count. Including himself and Rachel there were now six men and six women, ranging from Fong's and Cherry's thirty-something to Lolly Paringo and Esme Crown, who were twenty-one. It wasn't a bad sample, he thought, though their aptitudes and talents that had been useful and interesting in the sim might be irrelevant in the tanking experiments. Would Cherry York's encyclopaedic knowledge of Neolithic civilisation, Field Shaloman's skill at midwifery, and Martin Fong's facility with invention and mechanics make them any more or less viable for spending time in a stas-tank? Would his own skills and attributes be of any use? Lolly and Esme with their flexible physicality might not do well with enforced inactivity — he was thankful he'd shared his self-hypnosis techniques with them all. That would definitely be of benefit.

"I hope they'll be okay," Rachel murmured.

"You mean you hope *we* will, surely," Cherry quipped.

"No — them. What if they change their minds? Gen already has once. What do you think, Til?"

"I think I'll miss her," the historian said quietly.

Cherry shrugged. "So will we all. I hope they don't regret this. I also hope *we* don't."

Seated in the claustrophobic vehicle, travelling to an unknown destination for an unknown period of time, Harry reminded the group of the skills they had developed with his assistance.

Rachel didn't.

He wished he had persisted with training her in the self-hypnosis instead of taking the shortcut of putting her under himself. It had eased her headaches, but she had never learned —

This is not the sim. She won't have headaches.

"Should have brought a book," Lolly said abruptly. "Oh — that's right. According to Chavez, I probably can't read."

Ho put his hand on hers and gave it a squeeze. "He implied I couldn't tie my own shoelaces."

"Your what?"

"Shoelaces," Til Lund said. "Long strips of fabric that used to be employed as shoe fastenings."

"Oh, those." Lolly nodded her comprehension. She added, vaguely, "Aiglets — or were those the big sleeves on dresses?"

"They were gigots," Til said with a tiny edge to his voice.

"When all this is over, I will knit you some," Ho said kindly.

"They didn't give us time to bring books," Rachel put in.

"Unseemly rushing," Fong suggested. "They have form for that. They tossed us into the sim with twelve hours' notice."

Harry said, "It goes further than that. They want us not to have any extra-mental source of entertainment."

"Why? What's the point? I can see why we weren't given entertainment in the sim — it was to make us fall back on one another — but tanking is a different matter."

"We won't be able to read in the tank in any case," Esme said.

Harry grinned at her. "Very true. As I expect we'll find out."

He'd been a bit dismayed to note the truck was fitted with toilet facilities, food, and water supplies, implying their trip might be a long one, but after what he thought was probably no more than five hours, they were let out inside a walled compound.

"This probably used to be a sports facility," Esme said. "Football or something like that."

Harry agreed. Outward Bound had a habit of repurposing venues originally built for other uses. The island motel had been a case of that.

He wondered if the stas-tanks they'd be using might have been repurposed too—maybe they'd once been beer barrels or pickling vats.

He was entertaining himself with the notion of pickled test subjects when the unsettling Doctor Darling emerged from the truck.

"DDD on your six," Rachel muttered.

The man looked them over with his odd pale eyes. "Welcome to the stas-tank project, elites."

CHAPTER NINE: DARLING, 2235

The first stop on this new adventure was a tour of the facility.

Harry was amused at how commonplace it seemed. They were to be the vanguard of subjects for the experiment that would allow *Elysian Dawn* to take them to the stars, but they were being treated like visiting dignitaries or possible investors.

He supposed that last notion wasn't too far from the truth. They were investing their futures, taking their chances, betting on their ability to survive.

His ideas of repurposed barrels were, not surprisingly, nonsense. The stas-tanks were purpose-built, using the same hardware and outer appearance as the tanks he was familiar with in medicine.

Like most physicians, he had been tanked before, as part of his training. Just as historical soldiers had been deliberately exposed to tear gas and the knowledge of psychological interrogation techniques, trainee medics routinely spent twenty-four hours in a tank with little sensory input. Unlike some of his peers, Harry had enjoyed tanking. His ability to put himself into a trance while choosing and maintaining his level of awareness made the experience controllable. He had come out feeling refreshed and cheerful. Tanking, he considered, was as good as a holiday.

DDD was clearly pleased to have the chance to show off the facility, and he insisted on explaining the system as if to novices. Technically, all but Harry, Esme Crown, and Field

Shaloman *were* novices, but they had shared their knowledge with the others in the sim, so everyone understood the application as Harry and Field had experienced it.

When Darling paused for breath, Shaloman suggested they were more interested in the experimental tanking planned for them than in the therapeutic system that had been in use for some time.

"How, exactly, is it different?"

Darling seemed momentarily put out, as if his train of thought had been derailed, but he recovered and said, "Obviously there are differences, but basically the process is simply an advanced version of what is widely accepted as a very safe, versatile, and beneficial process."

"It's not, though," Harry said. "Therapeutic tanking has clear parameters regarding the time spent in the tank. Physically, prolonged immersion isn't too taxing, but the risks of remaining in the hypnotic trance for too long are quite well understood." He glanced at the others. "It's something like controlled fasting. A fast of up to sixteen hours is beneficial to most people. It gives the digestive system a rest and some find it sharpens the mind. Keep it up for too long, though, and the body starts to starve. The brain—"

Darling said quickly, "Although the new system is based on therapeutic tanking, there are marked differences. For example, therapeutic tanking is generally undertaken with hydration only. With the body at rest, the need for nutrients is low and—"

"You mean you would need to feed us in long-term tanking," Rachel said.

"Obviously." Darling didn't look at her.

"Have the level of nutrients and speed of delivery been calculated? How would the passing of extended time affect the integrity of the delivery system?" Rachel persisted.

"Needless to say, all that has been done. As I was saying,

with therapeutic tanking, the need for nutrients is low, and sensors report on any drop in blood sugar or variation in hydration, while—"

"That's therapeutic tanking," Esme Crown said loudly. Her voice sounded edgy. "We understand how that works, and we accept it's been thoroughly researched. Proof of concept is obvious. I've seen it in use, and Harry has undergone it."

"I have too," Field said.

"So," Esme persisted, "we need to know how thoroughly researched the long-term version has been. Please can you answer the question and stick to information regarding that?"

Darling was clearly not pleased, but he did as she asked.

After an hour of lecturing and repeated requests for clarification, Harry thought he understood the process—possibly more clearly than DDD would have liked.

Therapeutic tanking simply allowed the body and mind to rest and recover. The tanking developed for *Elysian Dawn* was altogether more rigorous. Instead of being in a light trance and vaguely aware of sound and vibration, the long-term tanked would be deeply asleep. Respiration would be slowed, and heart rate barely perceptible. In this state, the body would need drastically reduced nutrition and hydration. The brain would be unaware of anything, with no more than low-level maintenance activity.

Harry perceived that none of the viabilities liked the sound of this. He didn't care for it himself. How far back could consciousness retreat before it became unrecoverable?

"It will be very safe and highly economical," Darling went on. "With so little brain activity and with the bodily functions slowed, oxygenation is minimal, usual entropy is enormously retarded and—"

"How about muscle wastage?" Lolly enquired.

"That will obviously not be a problem."

"There's nothing obvious about it. You have only to look at an arm that's been in a cast for six weeks. And that's with normal nutrition and circulation — increased circulation at the point of injury."

Darling sighed. "We use a sophisticated exoskeleton. You may have heard of exer-sims. They are used by certain people with a pathological dislike of exercise to retrain the brain and to improve muscle strength without conscious effort."

"Doctor Darling, I've trained in an acro-sim and we have all used crop-sims in the simulation. So the tanks are fitted with a light version of those."

He nodded. "Only a small amount of stimulus will be necessary. Economy of effort at its finest. And of course the bio-equality-stasis-sustainability-environmental-fluid will provide the optimum environment."

"How do we wake up?" Field asked.

"The facility staff will monitor all subjects closely throughout the test periods and will guide you in and out of the stasis state."

"That's what happens here, but what about when we're on *Elysian Dawn*? There will be no facility staff on Magellan Sixteen."

"Well, obviously." Darling gave a short laugh that was almost a scoff. "The system is fully automated. It will be integrated with the intelligent FeTtL drive. As you will be aware, there will be no captain and crew to fly the ship." He held up a hand as though to deflect responses. "It has long been understood that unpiloted ships, land vehicles, and aerial travellers are far safer than those controlled by humans. They make allowances and adjustments, and an autopilot never has an unexpected encounter with a wasp." He waited for a laugh that didn't come.

"The onboard computer will automatically begin the revivification process when the ship reaches orbit around the destination planet, giving you several months to reach normal alertness and to reorient yourselves." He cast a chill gaze over them. "I trust you now understand the system?"

They nodded.

"How are the animals you tanked progressing?" Jonty Lane asked.

"I have not been concerned with that side of the facility," Darling said coolly. "If you wish to know the details, apply to Doctor Shah."

"How?"

Darling touched his wrist chip with alacrity. "Doctor Shah — do you have time to talk to the tank candidates about your animal experiments? You —"

He cut off as a young man shot into the facility as if pursued by arrows.

Chapter Ten: Shah, 2235

Doctor Shah was as small and round as DDD was lanky and angular, and his face shone with good humour.

"Marvellous! Come on, adventurers, I've been waiting forever to show you round." He flicked a farewell wave to DDD, who evinced no desire to accompany them, then shooed them all through the door from which he'd ejected himself and blew out his cheeks in a comical grimace.

"Okay, folks—if you survived O, you'll find me a stroll in the park. Cold fish, isn't he?"

No one answered. Harry supposed they were all trying to work out why Doctor Dash Darling should be referred to as O.

"This is not a psych test, or a trap, just an opinionated comment. Be assured, O doesn't like me any more than I like him, but that's purely personal. We can, and do, work together when necessary, and we respect one another's achievements, even if we differ a bit on how we view the details. He's a good enough fellow.

"But you've come to see the tanks." He indicated the ranked rows at the other side of the warehouse-sized room. The tanks varied in size and, unlike the ones Darling had shown them, these were full of viscous brown fluid and *alive*.

"Here are the stars of the show," Shah said, slapping two of the tanks in rapid succession. "In Number One we have Ned, aka Neddy, or Neddy Boy. He's a Shetland pony, and he's been tanked for almost a year." He paused and cast a sparkling look around the company. "Before we go into this, have we anyone here with more than common knowledge of

76

animal physiology?"

"I'm a vet," Jonty Lane said. "And the rest of us know at least as much as the usual lay person. We all dealt with animals in the sim for a year, though that was necessarily virtual."

Shah nodded. "Right! Hands-off husbandry. Wouldn't suit me. I like to get down and hands-on with my stock."

"We'd have preferred that."

"Who wouldn't? By the by, you might not have known, but the virtual goats and ducks you husbanded in the sim are some from my gang. So to speak. Chav put it on me to give you whatever the designated gangsters produced. Mind, if you'd been parsimonious with the feeding I *might* have been tempted to short-change you on the wool, eggs, and milk. Luckily, you weren't. I warned Chav I *would* give them extra food if you fell down on the job." He gave them a somewhat feral grin and added, "Unfortunately, you're a bit hands-off with Neddy Boy as well. See if you can spot him."

Harry peered in through the visualisation window. At first the fluid seemed opaque, but after a few seconds he detected a solid shape floating inside.

"He's very small," Jonty said doubtfully.

"We thought he was a well-grown specimen," Shah said. "I assure you he was in optimum condition when he entered the tank. I wouldn't have it otherwise. My gangsters have to score ninety-seven at least before I'll even put them on the waiting list. Even then most of them wind up as controls. They're all properly socialised and loved." He patted the tank again.

"He's tiny even for a yearling—he's more like a Falabella," Jonty said.

"Oh!" Shah's face creased in a grin. "I assure you he's not a Falabella. His dam—Lucy Jay—is nine hands and his sire, Mister Peebles, is a little taller. When fully grown he should be something in that region. I have the exact calculations if you want to see. But I think you're under a misapprehension. Although he was foaled fifteen months ago, Neddy Boy is developmentally a tad under four months old. Give him another few months and he'll be younger than his younger sibling, Jack Sprat."

"Doesn't he age and grow at all?" Jonty sounded puzzled.

"He is aging, but—let me see. If we take the rather simplistic ratio of one to three hundred and sixty . . . or one day per year . . . he is now a little less than a day older than the day he was entrusted to the tank." He patted the tank again with what seemed like affection and touched a small panel. "Here—this is a holo of the way he looked on that day. That's him with my kid Willow. Very attached. Will wanted to tank with him, but I compromised by giving Ned this holo to keep him company."

Harry stared at the pony foal, pictured nuzzling at a round-faced girl child.

"You did this to make your daughter happy?" Rachel asked.

"Yes—and for the staff here. The idea is to make sure they *never* forget Neddy Boy is a real pony with personality and practical value. We all talk to him. He can't hear us, but he can never be Subject Six-Oh-Five. Not while I'm in charge." For a moment, his face went steely, then his smile returned. "We name our gangsters and register the names. Each has a file, listing everything up to and including favourite foods.

"Once Ned's out of the tank, he'll start growing and aging just as if he'd never been tanked. Our other star, here"—he touched the second tank again—"is Toodles Oswald Anderson Doe . . . or Toad for short." He laughed. "Toodles actually is a toad, and he has been held in this tank for ten years. He predates this facility. Would you like to meet him?"

Jonty nodded, wide-eyed.

"Grand! I'll start the revivification and we'll come back in a few hours. We wake him up once a year for a few tests and some R-and-R. That includes a snack of mealworms and once some time with a lady toad we call Hithere. Some of the offspring are in the Toad Abode ... We wait until the mealworms pass through his system before we pop him back in the tank, of course. There's strictly no re-tanking with food in the system. That's one reason we generally tank or re-tank at the end of a natural sleep period."

Jonty said, "Do you have any animals that have already come out of the tanks permanently?"

"Oh, surely! Come on and meet the gang!"

Still talking volubly, Shah led them out through an airlock to a green paddock planted with shade trees. It was divided into six equal pens, each with a water trough and stable and a mix of vegetation.

"Grab some carrots from that bin," Shah said, waving to a wooden barrel. He whistled sharply.

Ponies, goats, and a couple of cows in the nearest pen raised their heads from their grazing or browsing and sauntered over to the gate. They seemed pleased to see Shah, and one of the cows presented her head for a rub.

"This is Staz," Shah said, indicating a pony and offering a carrot with his left hand. "Foaled the same day as Ned to Mister P and Twinkle Jay — she's Lucy's sister. That makes Staz and Neddy half siblings on one side and first cousins on the other. She's his control, and a right little madam. Over there is Lollipop the goat. Her twin, Eep, is in Tank Six. Jess and Ice Cream are controls for —"

"Have any of these actually been in the tanks?" Harry asked.

"Not in this pen. The ex-tankies are over here." He moved on and indicated three brindled goats leaning on the fence in expectation of food. "Meet Ginger, Nutmeg, and Spice.

Nutmeg is a two-month veteran, Ginger did three, and Spice a couple of weeks, twice over. Their controls are Apple, Mush, and Pear, just through the gate. My daughter named Apple.

"Feel free to go into the pens. Feed them carrots, check them over—give 'em a hug if you want. They love hugs. I can give you a stethoscope if you want to do a heart check and you—vet—"

"Jonty," Jonty put in.

"Jonty, you can bring any of them in for a blood scan. No need for needles. They've got collar ports—totally painless, as I can attest." He shoved up the sleeve on his right arm and tapped a white sensor. "This one talks to my chip and tells me off if I overindulge in carbs." He looked back to Jonty. "You can compare blood scans done at weekly intervals, before and after tanking. The variation is minimal."

Rachel said, "In your opinion, Doctor Shah, does tanking make any difference to your animals?"

"They're not too pleased at the fast needed before they go in, if we can't manage to catch the end of their sleep, but they come out raring to go."

Jonty said, "So they all survive with no ill effects."

"Exactly. The survivors are, as far as tests and observation will show us, exactly as healthy as their controls—though necessarily younger. The concept isn't all that new. Back in the twentieth century, fertilised embryos collected at the same time could be raised as children as much as a couple of years apart in age."

"That wasn't quite what I asked." Jonty sounded apologetic.

Shah sighed. "I know. You want the survival rates."

Jonty nodded. "Sorry."

"No need to be sorry." He pushed his hands through his hair, which was as ebullient as the rest of him. "I could give you a lot of official scientific claptrap, but I won't."

They waited.

Shah sighed again. "The survival rates for the first subjects weren't as good as I would have liked. We — I — because I am the one responsible for this program — put some of our animals through therapeutic tanking. Our poster child is Annie — over there, see?" He indicated a dappled Shetland mare drowsing in the sun. "Annie has been tanked fifty times and she doesn't even nip me when I approach her with the halter. Annie had a sister named Vera, two years older, from the same dam and sire. We used Vera for the first large tank subject. We'd been successful with Toodles, you see, and with a couple of rats. You can't meet them because they're gone from perfectly natural lifespan issues — mind, we do have a nine-year-old rat called Rani, but she's still tanked. Vera was seven, full grown but smaller than Annie. She'd gone through the thera-tank, no problems, so we were confident when we popped her in the long termer. We gave her a week."

"She didn't survive it?" Harry prompted.

"No. Neither did Pence and Jam, a couple of dorper sheep. I was ready to pull the plug, but the two goats, Nan and Papa who went it at the same time, came out of it lively as you like. That gave us hope and we tried once more — and we've had no more losses. Oh, we've had animals who've died, but since Vera, Pence and Jam, not one of those deaths has been directly attributable to tanking. Not even indirectly, except in as much as Cassie, who choked on an apple, might not have been given one if she hadn't been at this facility. She survived, by the way, but it was a near thing. Nowadays apples are *always* cut before feeding. We learn from our errors, and we do our damnedest not to make them in the first place." He spread his hands. "I'd say the chances of surviving a tank are at least as high as surviving a common food you had never happened to eat before and which you had no reason to believe was unsafe for you."

"You'd tank yourself? Or your daughter?" Rachel asked.

"Me? Not on your life. Been in a thera-tank and didn't like it. If I went into a long-termer, how could I trust O not to tinker with the mechanics?" He stared them down and laughed. "Joke, joke. But I will *not* take my eye off the ball. This place runs on *my* law, and if I'm unavailable, Zeus alone knows who might start taking shortcuts or referring to Annie as Subject Zed-Nine-Two. I never will."

"That's not—"

"I *know*. You want to know if I'd tank Willow. The answer is no, and so I told her when she wanted to go in with Ned. I had to threaten to ban her from visiting if she didn't stop plotting to crawl in with him. Even telling her there was no way I would let her into even a thera-tank didn't work. No. But it's probably not for the reason you think. Objectively, I'd say Wills would tank at least as well as Toodles and Annie, but there's one major barrier."

"She's your child," Rachel said.

"Yes, and I love her to bits, even when she's calling me all the names under the sunshine for tanking Neddy without her. It's been a year, more or less, and she's still giving me the evil eye when she remembers. But that's not the point. She's seven. Seven going on thirty, but still chronologically seven. That means another nine years before she could be tanked without my consent. Even if I gave my consent, it's probable I'd lose my job. In eleven years, I won't get a say. Mind, Neddy Boy will be out long before then." He looked from Rachel to Lolly Paringo. Harry knew Lolly was a few months older than her friend Esme, but she didn't look it. "I trust you are emancipated Ms—"

"Loralie . . . Lolly. And I am." She spread her hands. "I got emancipated when I was a kid—and signed up with Cirque du Sud. 'Bats like me get special dispensation, because if we waited to begin training at the normal emancie age, we'd be too old physically."

Shah looked horrified. "Please, don't mention that to Willow!"

"I won't. Anyway, I'm twenty-one."

"Grand! Might I ask why you're not still with the Cirque du Sud?" He pronounced it as Serk dew Sud to rhyme with bud, to Harry's amusement. He *must* have been aware of the spelling to be able to do that, especially when Lolly had modelled the correct pronunciation.

Lolly shook her head dolefully. "Aged out. Could have stayed on as a trainer, but I saw a banner-ad and — here I am. In any case, there are rumours that the Cirque will be closed down . . . if the intentional risk law comes in."

Shah raised his undisciplined brows. "It *is* in."

"What?"

"Passed six months ago. You must have been living under a rock . . . oh, you were in the sim."

Harry wondered what else they might have missed. "Doctor Shah . . . " He tapped his chest. "I'm Harry, by the way. If the intentional risk ban is now law, how is it that Outward Bound is still allowed to proceed?"

"Friends in high places — shareholders with a vested interest. Grandfather clause. Take your pick. Personally, I think the Grandfather is the most likely. You signed up *before* the legislation, and *Elysian Dawn* is already legal. So, because you're all old enough to give informed consent, and since you have all been given full disclosure, it's all systems go. Anyway, on the record. I wouldn't get in a tank, and I won't let Willow, but my wife, Inge, will be first in line once the volunteers — you — have gone through the first tests."

"Why hasn't she done it before?" Field asked gently.

"Obviously, she wants to make sure it's as safe as we believe it is. You see, she has an inoperable tumour. She can live with it for a few years more, but eventually we'll lose her . . .

she's opted for cure-coasting as soon as it's approved, which we both hope is very soon. She says she has to choose between watching Willow grow up and seeing her *as* a grown up. The sooner we get her into stas, the less damage that tumour will be able to do and the better the chances of a cure working when one is available."

He looked tired. "Now — you understand that I have more than a professional investment in this. I'm betting my Inge's life on it working."

After a short silence, Rachel ventured, "Will we be using the tanks back there?" She pointed back into the warehouse.

"You'll be using tanks made to the same specs, except for the shape. Ours are typically deeper to allow for quadruped legs. Now — it's probably lunch time. I think Cat and Bindi have plans to feed you all in the big hall, then you can come back and spend more time with the gang and meet Toodles and your virtual goats and ducks, which are in the back paddock. Meanwhile, if you come up with any more questions, remember them so you can ask me. I'm no expert on humans, but I know the gang inside out, and I know my way round the tanks. I'm there for the prep, and the tanking, the monitoring and the extraction, so I see it all from go to whoa. Okay?"

They assented, and Field and Jonty let themselves into the pens. Harry watched. He wasn't an expert on animals, but to his untrained gaze the gang, as Shah referred to them, looked healthy and happy.

"I wish *he* was in charge of tanking us instead of DDD," Rachel said.

So did Harry.

"O," Lolly said. "Why O?"

"For Doctor Dash Darling?" Harry grinned. "I think the clue lies in the middle name and the initials. DDD- D-Dash-D . . . Dash Dash Dash. Morse code."

Lolly looked no more enlightened.

Chapter Eleven: Tanked, 2235

After three days at the tanking facility, the viabilities were returned to Brierly Island, where they remained for a further six months. This time, they were given seeds, more tools, and a small flock of goats and ducks. Every week Chavez came to visit them, bringing with him a guest who specialised in practical skills. Everyone was obliged to participate in these classes, whether they had any aptitude for the subject or not.

They had all practised many of these skills in the sim, but reality was not the same. As Harry put it, chopping down a tree in the sim was hard, blister-inducing work, but there was *no* danger of a branch snapping off and falling on anyone.

Milking goats that didn't necessarily want to be milked was also different, but Jonty professed herself pleased to get some hands-on animal experience. Field helped out when kids were born, on the same grounds.

Life on the island was enjoyable for everyone except Williams, who said he felt his computer skills were going to waste. Harry wondered if he might drop out of the program as the realisation dawned that he'd have to decide soon before it was too late to catch up on the rapidly changing digital world. There was also the fact that his skills would become obsolete if he shipped out.

Shoulders of Giants. The infrastructure for the digital world would not exist on Magellan Sixteen.

Once that occurred to Harry, he began to wonder about the rest of the viabilities and their skills. Lolly and Esme would presumably pass on their physical excellence to the next generation of children, either by inheritance or by training and example. Rachel's job as a nutritionist would be doubly valuable while negotiating new foods on a new world. His counselling would be useful, along with his background in exotic diseases, as would Field's expertise with babies and Jonty Lane's with animals, but what about the others?

Cherry York and Til Lund were historians, and Harry wondered how relevant these disciplines would be when they were so far from the places and events they had studied. *They who don't listen to history are doomed to repeat it . . .* or something . . . but would that pertain on another world?

Sofia Kataranga was a geologist—that was useful. Ho was a physicist who could also spin and knit.

Harry closed down his speculation. He'd been thinking it was down to the viabilities, but there would be hundreds— thousands—more settlers. Their drop would be lost in an ocean of people. There would be hundreds who shared at least some of their talents, and hundreds who had other talents they lacked.

He wished he could have checked in with Flavia and Harley before heading to the island, but there had been no chance. His chip, along with those of the others, was dormant, so he couldn't check his funds balance or anything else. He was glad he'd transferred all the available money to Flavia and he hoped she was using it as necessary for herself and Turq.

He tried to visualise Turq as a clean child, shining with scrubbing and sufficient water and more food. Maybe they'd got a pet dog. Turq would like that.

He'd love to have seen his godchild growing and thriving . . . but her prospects hinged on his *not* being able to see her.

Well, he'd warned Flav he might not be able to visit.

It occurred to him that the viabilities might never be allowed to contact anyone outside the program before they finally shipped out—but that was nonsense. No one had tried to prevent the five departed viabilities from leaving. They weren't prisoners. They were volunteers.

In late August, Chavez arrived alone to inform them they were going to the facility for the first tanking experiment.

"Leave everything," he said in his harsh voice.

"When are we coming back here?" Sofia asked. She'd dug up some clay and was modelling plates.

"That depends on how the trials go," Chavez said. "In any case, you won't be needing anything from here."

"The goats and ducks need caring for," Jonty informed him.

Chavez seemed surprised, and Harry thought he genuinely hadn't considered that. In theory, the creatures could fend for themselves, but they were penned to keep them out of the crops.

Williams said, "I'll stay on with them, Jonty. I'd almost decided to pull out anyway. I'll stay until you get through the testing and can make other arrangements."

"Me too," Lolly said abruptly. She smiled at Esme's shocked expression. "Remember what Tyler said? Tired of being led around in a hood? Besides, anyone who can forget to provide care for the goats and ducks isn't someone I particularly want to trust with my life. See you when you come back. And Sof, I'll clear up your potting."

Chavez's cold features showed no change, and he made no other suggestions but waited with badly concealed impatience while Sofia got the clay off her hands and arms and Til removed the pottage he was making from the trivet over the fire.

The other viabilities got solemnly onto the boat and waved to the two left behind until the cold spray sent them into the cabin.

Rachel sat down and stretched her legs, tucking one arm around Harry. "Then there were ten," she intoned.

Again they travelled in the truck, which this time collected them from the port.

Again they were decanted in the repurposed sports ground, where Doctor Darling came to meet them.

Bindilina Ash was there as well, but Cataleya Conti and Bao Woo had not made the trip.

Ash smiled and greeted them with enthusiasm. "I hope you had breakfast," she said.

"Not yet. We were carried off without any warning." Esme sounded hopeful.

Ash said, "Well, that's probably to the good. You'll be able to enter the tank tomorrow morning instead of waiting out the fast. Doctor Darling will take you through to the final briefing."

"Don't we even get coffee?" Sofia quipped. The truck this time had been stocked only with water.

Ash shook her head. "Sorry folks, it might mess with the calculations."

They followed the chilly DDD into the tank room they had visited before, but there was no time to linger before each was put in the charge of a nurse in blue scrubs.

Harry barely had time to kiss Rachel goodbye.

He sat on an examination couch and awaited events.

The nurse looked at him gravely. He saw she had green eyes, but little more of her was visible, with mask and hair net covering most of her features.

"Good afternoon, Doctor Fejoa. My name is Amber Fordyce. I'm your prep nurse. Please pop into the shower while I go through your notes. Put on the gown provided afterwards." She indicated a sealed cubicle.

Harry showered, pleased to discover blue light and purgatives were not part of the preparation.

When he emerged, wearing an inadequate blue gown that was neither wide nor long enough for comfort, the nurse indicated a chair covered with a blue towel. In case of drips?

"Sit down, Doctor Fejoa. We just need to run through a few things . . . Full name?"

The questionnaire was almost identical to the one he had filled in initially. Fordyce appeared to be comparing answers, nodding now and again.

"Okay. I'm going to run through what's happening tomorrow. You will remain in this prep room for the rest of today. You may drink as much water as you want, but no food. This is standard procedure before any medical tests or scans."

"I know. I'm a physician."

"I understand that, but we have to do this by the book. You can go to sleep when you want. There is a temperature control on the wall and a cellular blanket in the press. In the morning, you'll be asked to sign a waiver and agreement, and to nominate a champion."

Harry held up a hand. "Now that, I don't understand."

She said, steadily, "A champion is a person who can advocate for you and make decisions on your behalf while you're in the tank. Think about who you would like to appoint."

"Rachel. She's my fiancée."

Fordyce sorted through some papers. "Would that be Rachel Traveller?"

"It would."

"She won't be considered suitable, because she is also a tank candidate."

"She's the person I want."

The green eyes narrowed. "I'll see what—"

Harry pointed at her. "Please don't say that. Just make it happen. If you're capable enough to be in your position, you should be capable of making a decision."

"Or you walk?"

"I might." He remembered what Lolly had said about trusting Chavez with her wellbeing. He added, "I probably won't. I've put a good deal of time into this project already, and I understand from Chavez—does he have another name?"

She nodded. "Landon Chavez."

"Right. I understand from him that walking now would compromise my and Rach's chances of shipping out."

"All right. I will put Ms Traveller down as your champion, although her advocacy would cut in *only* if you were incapacitated and she was conscious and available. But please, do appoint a second and third champion who will take over in the event that neither you nor Ms Traveller can act on your behalf."

Harry gave her Flavia's name and address then asked for Doctor Shah.

To his relief, Fordyce nodded approval. "Tav Shah is a good choice. He's the person I'd choose for myself if I were in your shoes.

"After you've finished the official paperwork, and given your declaration, you will be taken to the tank and fitted with a cannula. You will need to remove your clothing and prep your skin with a protective coating. That's not strictly necessary for a five-hour stint, but it will be practice for your next tanking. You can ask for a sedative, but that may render you unable to climb into the tank, which would result in aborting your program. You *must* enter the tank of your own volition and with no help or duress.

"Once inside, you will be plugged in and the stas drug will drop you quite quickly into stas. There you will remain—under constant observation—for five hours, at which time you'll be revived and asked to climb out and shower. Debriefing will follow, during which you may be asked the same questions we have covered here, or other questions which may seem nonsensical to you. Please do answer these to the best of your ability. Don't — er — " For the first time, she faltered.

"Don't try to be smart," Harry said drily.

"Exactly. I personally assure you any question, no matter how personal or seemingly irrelevant, will be asked with your wellbeing in mind. Okay?"

"Yes."

"Any questions?"

"Not at this stage. You've been surprisingly forthcoming."

"Thank you. That's all, officially, but off the record, remember you can change your mind at any point up to the administration of the stas drug. You are a volunteer."

"I'm being paid."

"That's immaterial." She gave him a quick smile — or he thought she did from the way her eyes crinkled — got up and left the room.

Harry lay down with his hands behind his head. He missed Rachel.

He spent the night in a soft trance and came out of it when someone tapped and entered the room.

"Nurse Fordyce?"

"That's right. Are you ready?"

"I am." Harry got off the bed.

"I've brought the waiver and agreement for you, and I contacted your three champions-elect, all of whom agreed to act for you. You may be interested to know that your fiancée has nominated you and Doctor Shah as well. Her third choice is Abra Kiev, who has left the program voluntarily, but who presumably knows what needing to act for you would imply.

"Take a few moments to read these papers and sign when you're ready. You'll need to use a stylus. Your chip won't work."

"It hasn't worked since we went into the sim," Harry said.

"It has to stay powered down so as not to confuse it when

you enter stas."

"It wouldn't do to have it report my departure from this life, I suppose."

"Exactly."

Harry read the waiver and agreement. They were clearer than he expected, and he noted the board had hired someone with word sense to write them.

Finally.

He signed.

Amber Fordyce signed across his name.

"Are you one of the directors? Or on the board?" he asked.

"No. I'm an employee. Unofficially, I am also Doctor Shah's sister-in-law. Inge, his wife, is my elder sister. So you see I have a strong interest in the success of this trial. I genuinely wish you well, Doctor Fejoa, and not only for your sake but for my sister's."

Harry nodded his understanding. Cure-coasting was not the point of these tests, but it was clearly a side hustle. He wondered how much Shah and his wife had taken the differences in their health status into account. He and the other viabilities were all in optimum health and condition.

He got up and followed Fordyce from the cubicle, smiling at Rachel who was emerging from a cubicle with her own nurse.

"You look better in a paper gown than I do," he called.

"I should hope so! I also should hope we get some dinner tonight."

"Maybe we can have room service," Harry suggested. "Or go out on the town."

"I wish."

They were ushered with the others and their nurse attendants to the tank room. In the months since they'd seen it, there had been a transformation. The tanks were now separated into alcoves, each with an opaque screen.

Chavez and DDD awaited, apparently to give the final

briefing.

It was a pity his two least favourite people were there, Harry thought.

It was mercifully brief, mainly a reiteration of the things Amber Fordyce had already explained.

"Is everyone ready to proceed?" Chavez asked.

The viabilities exchanged glances among themselves. Harry saw Esme biting her lip and twisting her hands together.

Ho must have seen it too, because he moved over to stand beside her.

His move triggered the others, who shifted into a huddle.

Harry felt Rachel tuck her arm around him. "Ready?" she whispered.

"I am. But if you're not—"

"I am. We're having dinner together."

"Of course we are."

Chavez said, "If you're ready, please state the fact aloud for the record, then step into the tank cubicle. Remove your clothing and, if you wish, immerse yourselves in the preparation lotion. When ready, touch the screen in your cubicle and Doctor Darling will hook you up."

Harry felt Rachel squeeze his hand. "Last one in's a rotten egg."

He laughed and kissed her. Then he said, "I, Harrison Fejoa, state for the record that I am ready to enter the tank for a period of five hours." He stepped forward.

Behind him, he heard Rachel stating her name. Then the others chimed in.

Inside the cubicle, he undid the tapes on the gown and hung it on the prosaic hook provided. The tub of preparation liquid looked uninviting, but he shrugged and stepped in, lying down to let the viscous blue fluid coat his skin. It was neither warm nor cold, reminding him unpleasantly of the goop he'd drunk before entering the sim.

He touched the screen and waited.

Nothing seemed to happen, but he realised he couldn't assume he would be the first.

Unsure how long he'd be waiting, he put himself into a light trance. His thoughts were of Rachel.

He hadn't nearly had enough of his cultivated daydream when the door opened and Darling stepped in. He wore a white coverall and hood which was streaked with a disturbing mix of the blue lotion and brown bio-fluid.

"Hold out your right wrist," he said without greeting.

Harry, quickly coming to alertness, did so.

"I'm about to insert a cannula. Its purpose is—"

"I know what a cannula is. We all do."

Harry held his arm steady while Darling swabbed it clear of the syrupy blue stuff, cuffed him, and put in the cannula. He worked efficiently and Harry was pleased to note his deftness.

He decided Darling was not a cruel man, despite his unfortunate manner.

"Thank you, Doctor Darling," he said.

The man's light eyes met his gaze and held. "I need to go through the instructions even though you undoubtedly know them already. Do you require a sedative?"

"No thanks. "

"I didn't think you would. Your pulse is steady. I'm going to lift the lid. Three steps will appear. Please use them to get into the tank."

Harry complied, stepping down without hesitation into the thick brown soup. "No exoskeleton?" he queried.

"That's not necessary for five hours."

"I understand. I take it I lie down the same as I did when I used the thera-tank?"

"Almost. In this case your face will be under the liquid. Do not submerge until you feel the stas drug taking effect."

Harry felt his brows go up. Somehow, no one had told him of this refinement.

Well, I didn't ask, he thought.

"The bio-fluid fills my lungs?"

"Yes."

He didn't like the sound of that.

"What happens when it's time to get out?"

"The fluid will be sucked out. After that there may be a coughing spell," Darling said. "I understand it's not a pleasant sensation when the subject is awake, but my colleague Shah suggests the animal subjects show no undue distress."

I wish Shah had told me that, Harry thought. He wondered how Rachel would take the news . . . or had taken, perhaps. "Am I the first to tank?" he asked.

"Esme Crown was the first scheduled. After you comes Martin Fong."

"Alphabetical order by surname. Okay." Harry let himself down to float in the bio-fluid. His right wrist rested in a groove. "Okay," he said again.

Darling nodded and reached for his wrist. "I'm introducing the stas drug now, Doctor Fejoa. Please count down from ten."

Harry felt a flush of warmth in his arm. "Ten, ni—"

Chapter Twelve: Honeymoon Island, 2235

"It was so weird," Rachel said when she and Harry convened in the complex dining room for dinner.

Going out had not been feasible, not only because the debriefing had taken a long time, but also because the facility was not in a town.

Nevertheless, they were hungry enough to find the food on offer appetising if not especially appealing. As Rachel said, it made a change from the pottage that had been their main fare on the island.

"Though not a particularly good change," she added. "Our island pottage is always good and at least the ingredients are minimally processed."

Harry smiled into her eyes. She looked beautiful, he thought. Her cheeks were slightly flushed, and her skin glowed as if it had been buffed with velvet.

He bit his lip at the silly comparison, but he went on smiling.

"How do you mean—weird?"

"*Weird.* If I'd known ahead we had to breathe the stuff I'd have backed out, but it was all right. I thought about Toodles and Neddy Boy and those three goats, and I thought nice Doctor Shah wouldn't do something to them if it hurt. Besides, that pony, Annie, has been tanked fifty times, and if it had been upsetting she wouldn't be so placid."

Annie had been thera-tanked, not stas-tanked, but Harry

didn't remind Rachel of that fact.

"So what was weird?" he asked again.

Rachel waved a forkful of a textured protein patty. "DDD asked me to count backwards and I started to and next thing, I was in my lovely emptiness." She smiled and clarified, "I mean the place you took me when I used to get headaches in the sim. I just lay there watching stars and clouds and waiting for the drug to kick in. Next thing . . . I was lying wrapped up in a towel and a nurse was offering to turn on the shower for me." She bit her lip lightly and gave him a rueful smile. "Harry, I meant, planned, and intended to think of you, but at least I got your nothing-place."

"How do you feel now?" he asked. He would *not* dwell on the fact she associated him with the emptiness of a foggy night sky. After all, she liked the place.

"Wonderful. The way I did when I woke up that first time you showed me the empty place. The only thing better would have been waking up with you." She belatedly inserted the forkful of food and chewed. "This is made of peas, mint, and tofu. It's quite good," she mumbled. She swallowed. "You look well too. You've got a bit more colour than usual and you look as if you've had a lovely rest somewhere and washed your face in buttermilk. I wonder if that's from the blue syrup or the brown soup? Whichever it is, they're really missing the market. People would pay well to get their hands on it."

Harry thought only Rachel could suggest using blue or brown goop as a beauty treatment.

"What did you see?" Rachel asked through another mouthful of the green protein compound.

"Nothing." He shrugged. "I intended to put myself into a trance and think of you, but I went out like that before I could do it." He clicked his fingers.

Out wasn't really the word, though. He had the confused memory of being deep, deep — then the wakening. He recalled

Doctor Darling mentioning coughing, but his throat and chest didn't hurt. He felt, as Rachel put it, wonderful.

Never mind the beauty aspect, he thought. This stuff could revolutionise mental health. Cure-coasting? It might well *be* a cure for some conditions.

"I seriously need to talk to Darling and Doctor Shah about that goop—Shah, mostly, because he's seen it working far more in practice," he said.

He intended to visit Shah that day, but after another round of debriefing and more cognitive and physical tests, they were taken to an island—not Brierly—where coconut palms grew and fish were plentiful.

It was a long way from anywhere, and although they worked to find food and to build shelters, it was more like a holiday. They swam and climbed rocks, kicked through rock pools and catalogued minerals, vegetation and wildlife. Harry wished he knew the name of the island and its geographical location, but although Sofia thought the rocks and soil composition gave her a few hints, none of them could do more than theorise.

"We need a botanist," Rachel said. "Anyone?"

The other seven, including Harry, shook their heads.

"I don't think Esme or Ho would have been much help with that," Rachel added.

Esme Crown and Khanh Ho had both decided not to proceed with the tanking. They had left the facility before Harry and the others emerged from their five hours in the tank.

Bindilina Ash assured Harry they had been cashed out, and that they had asked her to pass on their farewells.

Harry asked if they'd gone back to the island with Williams and Lolly, but Ash said she didn't know.

Exploring their new island was considerably more entertaining than their virtual exploration of the sim, and having ample available food meant they had no need to do much manual work.

It was a time to think, reflect, love and consider.

"I want to come back here for our honeymoon," Rachel said, snuggling up to Harry under a shade cloth they had made from palm leaves and fibres. They'd missed Ho for that—he was an innovative textile maker.

"That would be nice. When would you like to get married?" he asked. "We could always do it here and now."

Rachel said immediately, "I thought of that, but it wouldn't be official, so we'd have to do it again later. Let's pledge when all the tests are finished. Once we're married, I want to be with you always, and you know Chavez—he keeps putting us in separate cubicles. Thought! Let's ask for a double tank so we can spend the time together when we ship out."

"I wonder if *Chav's* married," Cherry York said, popping up from behind a large frangipani.

Rachel slapped her hand over her heart. "Lord, I hope not. His poor wife if he is."

"Yes. Martin and I have decided to get married before we ship out too," Cherry said.

Rachel giggled. "Don't tell Chavez. He'll take credit. He'll call us the 'Outward Bound Matchmaking Successes' or something."

Harry couldn't imagine Chavez saying anything like that, but he probably would take credit. He thought about the next tanking experiment, which was to last for six days. He hoped it wouldn't be too soon. He was interested in knowing how long the *tank euphoria,* as he and Rachel called their feeling of warm wellbeing, would last. He wanted to discuss it at length with Doctor Shah . . . what a pity Toodles, the longest tanker in history, was a toad. How could one measure euphoria in an amphibian?

He was thinking about this as he and Rachel walked along the beach hunting for seaweed that Rachel wanted to try for dinner when the sound of an engine approaching overhead alerted them to their imminent extraction.

Rachel sighed. "Damn it! I wanted to see if I could get that seaweed past Martin without him calling it *green muck*." She turned and walked towards the extraction point, which was a runway on the other side of the island. "Remember, we're coming back here, Harry Fejoa. You're on notice."

"We're coming back," Harry agreed. Then he added, "I wonder if anyone will tell us the name of this place, or will we have to prowl the Tropic of Capricorn until we find it?"

"I'm hereby naming it Honeymoon Island," Rachel said.

Chapter Thirteen: A Question of Engagement, 2236

The second tanking session felt quite routine to Harry. He and Rachel had made a pact to think about one another as they went under, even if just for a second.

The prepping was far less rigorous, and this time Darling had Harry hooked up within five minutes and with minimal conversation. Just before the stas drug was connected, Harry told Darling he wanted to visit Doctor Shah and his menagerie after they came out.

"Before you ship us somewhere else," he reiterated.

Darling nodded.

Harry was about to expound on his reasons when he saw Darling connect the vial and hastily thought of Rachel.

He was smiling as he went under and still smiling when he woke, as before, wrapped in a towel. He had no memory of emerging from the tank or of coughing up the last of the bio-fluid, and again he felt energised and full of hope and ideas.

He was emerging from the shower when Rachel shoved him back under the spray. "Did you think of me?" she demanded, pinning him to the back wall.

Showers were definitely a novelty for the viability team.

"I told you I would."

"I told you *I* would, and I did . . . before I went to my empty place again." She leaned against him and spluttered as the water ran down their faces.

"Are you supposed to be here?" Harry asked.

"Who cares? We're not children. We're not prisoners. We're volunteers." She kissed him with every sentence, then drew her face back to ask, "What are we doing today?"

"Debriefing, I suppose, then food, and I'm going to see Doctor Shah. Want to come?"

"Food first. And of course. I expect Jonty will come too. She's missing the goats from Brierly Island. And if she comes, Field and Sofe will too." She kissed him again, more thoroughly. "And if they come, Cherry and Martin will—and Til." She sighed. "Poor Til."

"Poor Til?"

"He and Genevieve were always partnered up in the sim and on the island. He must miss her."

"Well, I miss Lolly," Harry said. "She was fun."

"She was, wasn't she? Losing her and Esme was a blow."

Harry nodded. The youngest members of the team had always been entertaining and innovative. He hoped they'd find a way to continue their friendship and that their sim-pay was enough to set them up with something they wanted to do. He also hoped they wouldn't be docked part of the pay for their six months on the island.

He depressed the switch that turned off the recycling shower and grabbed a towel to wrap around Rachel. "I want to get you an engagement ring."

"After we finish the tanking—they'd make me take it off."

That was true.

"In fact, I won't be able to wear it while we ship out, either."

"So, you don't want one?"

"Yes, I do," she retorted. "I've calculated that *Elysian Dawn* will ship out in around twenty-two fifty-four—Chavez said no more than twenty years—but we'll probably be put in stas a few months beforehand, or even earlier. We still have the next two tankings, and if they're a few months apart . . . " She paused to calculate. "I think we can get married around twenty-two forty-two. That gives us time for our children to reach ten or so before we leave. They'll be old enough to understand what's happening and why." She paused again. "Harry."

"Yes?"

"*Can* children be tanked?"

"Yes," he said.

"Are you sure?"

"Certainly. Neddy Boy is a foal, remember."

"But what about the disclaimers? Remember what Doctor Shah said about his daughter."

Harry frowned. "Yes . . . but that was when human tanking was theoretical. Now it's proved to be safe and beneficial with eight of us tanked twice. Unemancipated children would be covered by their parents' disclaimer, though I'm sure they'd have to be named specifically on the document."

Rachel began to pat herself dry. "Good. You're right, of course. We'll be shipping out as a family unit. We'll have to ask for a tank-for-four."

They dressed in the provided clothing and left the cubicle hand-in-hand.

"You two look cosy," someone said.

Rachel turned and grinned. "Hello, Amber."

Amber Fordyce looked very different without her blue scrubs and mask. Harry looked her over appreciatively. She was blonde, curvy, and exactly his type. Or she had been, before Rachel.

He stifled a laugh at the thought.

"What?" Rachel dug him in the ribs. "Sorry, Amber. We're still on tank euphoria."

"I'm glad you're enjoying yourselves. Hungry?"

"Yes," Rachel said.

"Good. I've been asked to take you to my sister's place for

lunch. She wants to talk to you."

"That's lucky, because *we* want to talk to Doctor Shah," Rachel said.

"Come on, then."

"Don't we have to debrief?"

"Yes. Isn't it lucky I'm assigned to do that with both of you? We can take care of it after lunch." She paused a beat and said, "And in case you're wondering, I got the nod from Doctor Dash."

"How?" Rachel asked.

"I may have suggested he'll run out of elites to tank if he doesn't start taking your wishes into account."

"There are still eight of us," Harry said.

"Probably. I think Doctor Lund is on shaky ground."

Rachel said, "We know he's not happy that Genevieve dropped out, but surely he can see her at some point."

Fordyce shrugged. "Not my department, but I'll suggest it." She opened the airlock door that led out of the tanking facility and into Doctor Shah's domain.

Rachel stopped short. "We were going to invite the others to come."

"They're dining at the facility," Fordyce said. "They can join us later if they want."

Harry tugged Rachel's arm, but she disengaged and walked to the animal tanks. Unlike the ones they used, these were still in a rank instead of screened off.

"How's Neddy?"

"Fine, as far as we can tell," Fordyce said. She followed Rachel and laid her hand on the small window. "Hang in there, Neddy Boy. Only another year to go." She patted the small tank to her left. "Toodles. Hope you're dreaming of mealworms and lady toads."

"We don't dream," Harry said.

Rachel turned and stared at him. "Don't you? *I* do."

"What?"

"I told you I go to my nothing-place."

"That doesn't sound very enjoyable," Fordyce said.

"It is — it's a gorgeous clear emptiness that rests my soul. Harry gave it to me."

"That's not a dream," Harry said.

"It is so."

"Maybe for a second or so —"

"Much longer than that! I —" Rachel broke off as the first tank made a small hum. "What's wrong?"

"Nothing. It's just Neddy getting his exercise."

Rachel peered through the screen. Harry, moving behind her could see little through the brown fluid.

"He's galloping!" Rachel sounded entranced. "In ultra-slow motion, I mean."

"It's a gentle program to keep his muscles in shape," Fordyce said. "That was one of the errors Tav made with Vera. He's never stopped regretting that. Rani is fine because she had a little exoskeleton . . . Tav calls it the *rat-wheel*."

Rani, Harry recalled, was the tanked rat Doctor Shah had mentioned. "She's out of the tank?"

"Yes, she came out a few weeks back. Tav's got her up at the house in a giant rat palace so he can watch her. He's monitoring her in real time to see if her chronological age starts to creep up faster than the post-tank calendar suggests."

"And has it?"

"No. If anything, she's in better health than when she went in. Not that she's immortal, but she's aging normally. She was tanked at three months old, spent nine years in the tank and now functions as a perfectly normal six-month old doe. We introduced her to Caesar a while ago and they have a litter . . . What?"

"At six months?"

"Rats breed from about four months onwards and typically

stop at a year old. Rani's litter is average in number and composition." She smiled and tapped Rachel lightly on the wrist. "Tav thought it necessary to test whether breeding cycles would be disrupted by prolonged tanking. Of course one rat isn't a large sample, but three of our nannies have kids, and Annie is in foal." She turned away from the tanks and conducted them out past the animal paddock where several of the inhabitants looked up hopefully.

"Carrots after lunch, you lot," Fordyce called, laughing. "Too many and you'll all look like cartoons."

Doctor Shah lived in a pleasantly ramshackle house at the far side of the paddocks, separated from them by an undisciplined garden where ornamentals and eatable plants grew in mad profusion.

He was in the garden pulling spent pea vines when Harry and Rachel arrived with their escort. He straightened up and gave them a wide grin in greeting. "Welcome back, tankers! Hope you're hungry."

"We are," Rachel assured him.

"Grand. Before I take you in to meet Inge and Willow, I have a few questions. Amber . . . would you?"

"Sure." Amber Fordyce flicked them a wave and walked on towards the house.

"Right, thank you both for coming," Shah said hurriedly. "I know Inge wants to talk to you, and I'm asking you to answer any questions with absolute honesty and as much detail as you feel like giving. Don't worry about talking in front of Willow but please don't—" He shrugged and looked sheepish.

"Don't encourage her to want to try it for herself?"

"Exactly." He smiled. "I've told her Ned will be coming out in a year and assured her he won't have forgotten her. I just hope I'm right."

"He won't," Rachel assured him. "To us—to me—the six

days we spent in the tank was . . . um . . . borrowed time. I had dreams, but the time also passed in a flash. A bit like being in a trance. Harry can explain."

Harry explained how time could speed or slow when he went into a light trance, but he was sure he was telling Doctor Shah something he knew already.

"So you do dream?" Shah asked.

"I don't. At least, not that I remember. I blacked out as soon as the drug was connected and woke up a while after I was taken out of the tank. I have no memory of that, incidentally. Subjectively, I just opened my eyes a second after I closed them," Harry said.

"Interesting." Shah gave a half smile, very different from his usual ebullient grin. "I can run all the tests in the world, but nothing beats being able to ask someone who has experienced tanking and get an answer I understand."

CHAPTER FOURTEEN: INGE, 2236

Inge Shah—and there was an interesting name, Harry thought—was a paler, leaner, older version of her sister Amber.

Unlike Rachel, who was lean even when not suffering the effect of purging for the sim, Inge looked as if she should be rounder.

Harry thought he'd have known she was ill even if he hadn't been told. Nevertheless, she greeted him and Rachel cheerfully and invited her daughter Willow, who looked ridiculously like her father, to bring out the lunch she had made.

"She's a good cook," she said from her armchair on the veranda. "Basic stuff, anyway. I hope—"

Rachel said, "Basic is fine, Ms Shah. Harry and I and the others have been subsisting on basic food for a couple of years. The rations in the sim were the worst. Maybe that was deliberate, so we'd appreciate a radish and cucumber medley when we managed to grow some."

"We have a good garden here, which is useful since we don't live close to markets," Inge said. She turned as Willow came out, wheeling a trolley contraption of bread, vegetables raw and cooked, salads, and cheese.

"I thought you could serve yourselves," the child said. "That way you won't have to be polite and eat things you don't like."

"We'll like this," Rachel assured her.

Willow removed plates and forks from the undercarriage

of the trolley and handed them round. Then she loaded a plate for her mother and one for herself.

Doctor Shah beamed round and gestured to everyone to start.

They sat in a range of well-loved old chairs and ate.

Amber asked, casually, "You two as hungry as usual?"

"Hungrier, because the food is so good," Harry said.

The child looked him over. "Have you really not had any dinner for a week, Doctor Harry?"

"Really not, but it didn't seem very long to us."

"Dad says Neddy's not feeling hungry in the tank," Willow went on.

"I expect he's right. We didn't," Rachel said. She picked up a piece of bread. "Pumpkin bread! I haven't had this since I was a little girl."

Willow looked pleased. "I put some carrot in it too, and the green bits are parsley."

"Does everything taste the way you expect?" Amber Fordyce asked.

"Better," Rachel said.

Harry assumed she was complimenting the young cook, but he realised the food did taste uncommonly good. "I think my sense of smell is improved," he said.

"Can you quantify that?"

Willow's brows came down. "Am, why are you asking weird questions?"

Amber laughed. "I'm supposed to be doing a debriefing for Harry and Rachel, chick. It's part of my job."

"And it's our job to answer honestly," Harry said. He glanced at Amber. "When we finish, should we help to clear the plates?"

"Am and I will do that," Willow said. "Dad said you want to talk to Mum about the tanks. After that, you can come and see Rani and her babies. They looked like little pink blobs at first, but now they're pretty little ratlets."

With the meal finished, Amber helped Willow with the clean-up, and a few minutes later, the pair walked out with a basket of apples and lettuce, presumably to feed some of the animals.

Doctor Shah, who had said little during the meal, turned to Harry and Rachel then to his wife. "Inge, you can ask them anything you want. They've both been tanked twice, though only for a short time, and Harry already knew something about thera-tanking."

Inge turned to Harry. "How did that come about?"

"I learned about it in my medical training, and I've used it sometimes for trauma patients," he said. "I tried out the thera-tank for twenty-four hours while I was being trained."

"So you knew what to expect with Doctor Darling's tanks."

Harry shook his head. "I thought I knew, but a few things came as a surprise."

"Oh?" Shah said.

"I don't know whether it was deliberately left out of the briefing, but I hadn't realised we would be breathing the bio-fluid." He looked at Rachel. "I should have known, I guess. In thera-tanking, the participant's face is above the fluid level."

"I knew about that," Inge said. "It frightens me."

"The thought is frightening, but you don't go under until you've been put into stasis, so you're not aware of it."

"And we both woke up feeling marvellous," Harry put in.

Inge grimaced. "It's a long time since I've felt marvellous. You know I have an inoperable tumour. These things were supposed to have been cured a century ago, but now and again one is resistant to the treatment. Mine is one of those. My dilemma is this—on the one hand, I want to spend as much time with Tav and Willow as I can, but on the other I wonder how much damage it will do Willow to see me grow-ing weaker. I'm afraid she might blame herself later . . . or blame me. The other option is to enter stas sooner rather than later. I'm told that gives me a better chance in the long run. I won't be as weak, and the damage won't be as advanced. But—" She spread her hands. "You see my dilemma."

Harry said, "And *you* know it's your decision to make, Ms Shah. I'm sure Doctor Shah and your family will back you whatever you decide to do."

"Jam tomorrow," Rachel said. "That's what I'd go for. I know our situations aren't remotely the same, but Harry and I have elected not to buy rings and make things official until after we finish the tanking trials."

"But you two will be the same age," Inge said.

"Harry's a few years older than I am," Rachel said.

"I mean, you'll be the same age when you come out. I gather that when *I* come out—if I do, which wouldn't happen until a cure is developed—I would be the same age as I am now, more or less. In the meantime, Willow will grow up. She won't need me. She needs me *now*."

"She'll have me," Shah said. "And Amber."

"She'll also have you," Harry said as kindly as he could. "Ms Shah—"

"Inge."

"Inge, my parents died when I was not much older than Willow is now. I was taken in by a distant cousin who looked after me until I could manage alone. She was—and is—the kindest of people and I can never repay her, but there are things I will never know about my family. If my father or mother or both could be cure-coasting now, I'd have hope they could one day answer my questions. You're in the position to prepare Willow. Make voice messages for her, but tell her now who to apply to for information until you can be with her again. She will know you didn't abandon her for any reason but the hope of being there for her later."

Inge sighed. "Thank you." She glanced at her husband. "If

I take a year getting ready, do you think that would work?"

He nodded. "A year will give us a chance to study the longer-term effects." He looked apologetically at Harry and Rachel.

Rachel laughed. "We know we're guinea pigs. But Inge, I'm not frightened at all. We can come and see you again after our one-month stint if you like." She took Harry's hand and squeezed it. "Maybe you can come to our wedding. In any case, we'll come back to visit you before we ship out."

Willow and Amber returned soon after, and Harry and Rachel were introduced to Rani the rat and her offspring, then to the new kids.

As they returned to the human tanking part of the complex, Rachel said, "What you said about your parents—was that true?"

Harry gave her an oblique smile. "Maybe. I like to think that if they'd lived a few years more, we might have had a better relationship. It's true there are things I wish I could have asked them. I know almost nothing about Dad's family and not much more about Mum's. Flavia—my guardian until I was emancipated—doesn't know much either. She's a third cousin I'd met only once before the accident."

"Hm, I wonder if Willow knows how lucky she is to have parents who love her just as she is," Rachel said.

"We'll love our kids just as they are," Harry said. He thought of Harley Neal. Flav would do anything for Harley, despite having left the child's father before she was born. Harry had never known the details of that relationship, and he wasn't sure he wanted to.

Chapter Fifteen: Lessons from History, 2237

The month-long tanking passed in the flicker of an eye to Harry. He and Rachel were unable to visit Inge Shah as they had agreed because they were shipped out to Honeymoon Island again for almost a year, then fetched back and put in the tanks the same day.

Til Lund was no longer with them. He had gone to the island, but when Chavez and Darling visited for a six months' post-tanking check, he said he'd had enough.

For all the time Harry had known him he'd seen Til as a calm, friendly person, but he perceived there was a lot going on underneath. He was privy to Til's impromptu exit interview which happened unexpectedly and explosively. It began with *secretive* and *manipulative* and escalated to comparing Chavez and Outward Bound to various historical villains. *Megalomania* came up, along with *psychopathic*.

Harry stopped listening then. He was appalled that he'd missed the symptoms as Til grew increasingly quiet, yet he was fascinated by the accusations.

"He's not, is he?" Rachel whispered. "Chav, I mean."

"Psychopath? I doubt it. Sociopath, perhaps. He does have a dictatorial personality . . . oh, what do I know?"

"What do you think they'll do to him?" Cherry asked when the three had departed.

"Pay him off, the way they did the others," Martin Fong said with a shrug.

"But . . . did they?"

Cherry looked unnerved. Harry didn't blame her.

"Yes, they got the payments commensurate with the time they spent — sim, islands, tanking. That was agreed."

Harry nodded, hoping no one else would think of the notion that had crossed his mind. Inevitably, someone did.

Rachel said, "How do we *know* that happened? It's what we were told, but we didn't see the payments made, or see any of them again afterwards to verify if that was what happened."

"So what proof do we have Chavez won't shove Til out of the plane?" Cherry added. "History is full of promises being made and not honoured, and those in control coldly disposing of people who have become inconvenient or pulling some microscopic print up in a contract to prove they're not entitled to whatever it was they thought they'd get. What have we all had in common? Not just us and Til, but the others."

"We saw the banner-ads. We all have potentiality," Rachel supplied.

"And we acted on that," Martin said. He added, thoughtfully, "I was with a colleague when I saw the ad. He picked up on it, too, but he wasn't even mildly interested in following up. *Scam*, he said, then *rocks in your head* when I said I was going to apply."

"We all showed up and got through the initial interviews," Jonty put in.

They exchanged speculative glances.

"We're all fairly young," Field said. "What are the chances of twenty people — or seventeen if the phantom three never existed — being selected who were almost all under thirty-five?"

Harry pondered that. He recalled most of those whose interviews he had invigilated were skewed to the younger end of the spectrum. Maybe potentiality ceased to work as subjects aged. Or maybe, he amended, older people were less likely to act on it. They were probably settled in their lives and had ceased to seek opportunity and adventure. He remembered how Flavia had instantly shut down his suggestion that she and Turq might ship out. Her age had been her main objection . . . justified by her unlikeliness of having more children. Conti, too, had stated that she was too old. It hadn't seemed to disturb her.

Sofia frowned. "We all wanted to ship out—at least, initially. Though come to think of it, I'm not so sure about Abra and Paolo."

"That implies something else," Harry said, tracking on from his silent ruminations. "I'd say none of us had any strong ties with our lives at that point. We were all single. Abra has children and parents—but she was the first to leave. She and Steel bonded in the sim. Steel might have stayed if Abra hadn't made the move. I suspect his pull to be with her outweighed the pull of shipping out. I don't know about Paolo . . . but I suspect his main goal was to have his eyes corrected."

He gave Fong an apologetic glance. "I'm guessing you have no strong ties to your child, Martin?"

"None at all. I would have liked to have known him . . . or her . . . but it was the couple's request that I make my contribution and back gracefully away. And, before you ask, they offered to pay me off. I declined. Too much like human trafficking for my liking." He grinned. "If they ever happened to hear that I've shipped out, I should think they'll celebrate."

"That seems a bit extreme." Cherry sounded taken aback.

"I know. It shook me a bit at the time. The couple and I had been friends. I was initially under the impression I might be godfather or an honorary uncle, but"—he shrugged—"I was quickly corrected."

"You might have refused to be involved at all," Cherry

said.

"I might. Perhaps I should have. But I knew and they knew the chances of finding someone like me a second time was rare. By that, I mean the male half of the couple and I look similar and have similar IQs and interests. We work in the same areas. That's how we became friends in the first place. As far as I am aware we're not related, but our genetic profiles are alike. Our synchronicity was so marked we'd had to make a pact to stop saying *jinx*."

A tiny silence fell. Harry had time to wonder how he would have counselled the three adults in this situation or, indeed, the child when it grew to adulthood.

Field broke the silence. "Reverting to our own similarities, it seems that, apart from Abra and possibly Paolo, we were all willing to leave Terra on an adventure and not look back."

"And the corollary of that is?" Harry asked, arching his brows. He resisted the temptations to go into a jazz hands routine.

"We're not leaving anyone to — oh!"

"Oh," Harry said grimly. "Apart from Abra, none of us had or has devoted friends or family to ask questions."

"What about your cousin? The one who looked after you? I know you're fond of her," Rachel said.

"Flavia might have enquired if I disappeared from her radar as well as having my chip go dark, but I warned her I might be out of touch for quite a long time. Also, she has good and personal reasons to keep her head down. There is something hopeful though." He explained how he had got Chavez to release funds for Flavia's use. "He wasn't even difficult about it. I suggested I'd walk. He could have called my bluff, but he didn't even pretend to."

"Are you sure he didn't reverse the transfer after you came into the sim?" Cherry asked.

"We wouldn't know. Our chips were deactivated," Jonty

reminded.

Harry said, "I'm sure. I transferred the funds to Flavia immediately." He remembered he had officially made her his heir *and* his second champion. Outward Bound knew about her — even to her address, supposing she was still at his riverside apartment. "I made Flavia one of my champions after it was explained that Rachel might not be available at short notice," he said. "Amber Fordyce — my nurse — said she had let her know."

"And I made Abra Kiev one of mine. Amber told me she'd passed that on and that Abra had agreed. That suggests Abra really was paid off at least," Rachel said. She seemed to relax.

"If we trust your nurse," Cherry said darkly.

Harry tossed off the suspicious mood. "I do trust her. And I think Conti and Ash are honest, though in a pinch I'd trust Conti more. I also can't imagine Bao Woo bashing someone over the head and dumping the body, and he was the one who went off with Abra, Steel, and Paolo. He seems calm and balanced."

He thought of Til Lund, who had also seemed so quiet and balanced.

What do I know?

He added, "But most of all — you all met Doctor Shah, who has agreed to act for me and for Rachel. I would bet my last piece of pumpkin bread he has our best interests at heart."

"Would he know what happened to the ex-viabilities, though?" Cherry pushed.

"I don't know, but we can certainly ask him."

They had no more visits from Chavez until extraction when, as before, they were taken directly to the tanks.

This time, Harry was reasonably sure he was the first in line to be tanked. Since Esme Crown's abrupt departure, his was the first name, alphabetically speaking.

He had little time to wait before Darling came to hook him up. Not by a blink did the doctor suggest he remembered the blow-up on the island.

Harry submitted to having the cannula inserted, but before he climbed into the tank he asked, "Doctor Darling, what happened to Til Lund?"

Darling tilted his head. "He was extracted early, upon his own request. You were there and you know he left with us."

"What happened to him after that?"

"I assume he was paid out and allowed to leave. Why would you think otherwise?"

"I hoped that was what happened," Harry said.

"If that was the agreement, that was what happened, to the best of my knowledge." Darling surveyed Harry with his cold eyes. "With this doubt in your mind, do you wish to proceed?"

"Would you?"

"That's immaterial." Darling went on contemplating Harry. "Doctor Fejoa, it doesn't matter to me whether you proceed or not. You seem under the misapprehension that I am deeply invested in this venture."

"Aren't you?"

"Scientifically speaking, yes. I also hope the experiments go on being successful. I find the work here interesting and satisfying. I can also assure you I wish you all nothing but well. If not for you subjects, the work would be impossible. One can go only so far with animals that don't give verbal reports.

"On the other hand, I am an employee of Outward Bound. I'm paid for my time and expertise whether or not I tank you. If you want to speak with someone who is personally and maybe emotionally invested in this project, I commend you to my colleague Doctor Shah. He trusts the process. So does his wife. She is our first cure-coaster. I'm sure she would never have entered the tank if she hadn't seen the positive effect on you and the others."

Harry said nothing. He had assumed Inge Shah would have waited for the month-long experiment if not for the five-year one. Possibly, her condition had worsened. Or possibly she had jumped before she was pushed—so her husband and child would remember her while she was still moderately well.

"Yes or no?" Darling gestured at the tank. "If yes, you may enter the exoskeleton which you will be using this time around."

Harry stared at him. Cold fish, yes. Personality deficient—maybe. Yet he felt sure the man was being honest.

"Yes," he said. "But first—if I ask to contact my heir after this round, will I be able to?"

"Not through me, but if you apply to one of the board-members, you might be able to arrange something." The faint-est of smiles touched his angular face. "I commend you to Cat-aleya Conti. If anyone can arrange it, I would imagine she can. She works with small children, which need quite a lot of ar-rangements. I also believe that if she can, she will. She has a bit more humanity than some of those involved in this pro-ject."

He gestured at the tank again, and Harry climbed in. He aligned his limbs with the exoskeleton and pulled on the straps to tighten it. "I assume that's right?"

Darling bent to test the straps and nodded. Then he took hold of Harry's wrist, coolly, but not roughly. "I'm plugging you in in ten, nine . . ."

Harry relaxed, keeping just enough awareness to hold his head out of the liquid.

Rachel. I love—

—you.

Chapter Sixteen: Piggle, 2237

Having woken from his month in the tank, Harry was unsurprised when Rachel joined him in the shower. Subjectively, they had been together two hours before, but she greeted him as if it had indeed been a month.

"I love you," she said against his lips before spluttering. "Dang, I'll never get used to proper pressure in the showers. Are we going to see Inge today?"

Harry shook his head. "We can't. She went into the tank while we were on the island."

"Oh." She sounded disconcerted. Then she brightened. "We can still go to visit her the way Doctor Shah visits Neddy. But when did you find out?"

"I had a little talk with DDD before he plugged me in. He told me—no details, though."

Rachel snuggled in, averting her face from the water. "I've decided I quite like Doctor Dash. He's cold, but I think he's a decent person—or do I mean shy? He fits my cannula *after* I get in the tank."

Harry chuckled. "He doesn't mind me standing about naked and covered with blue jelly."

"No. He also asked if I wanted to have a haircut before I went in."

Harry caught the long dark tail Rachel's hair had become over their time together and combed his fingers through it. Even with it wet, he thought it felt silky and soft.

"I don't think the blue lotion is bad for hair."

"No, it conditions it. The bio-fluid isn't a problem either.

Anyway, I said I'd leave it. I might get a trim before we go in for the big five, though. Wouldn't want to wake up feeling like Rapunzel or Princess Melisande."

"That won't happen," Harry said, laughing.

"How do you know? Hair grows all the time."

"Yes, but we'll age about five days in the big five. That's not enough to notice. Hair grows less than half a millimetre in a day."

"I won't cut it then. I've just decided I want to go full-on Rapunzel for our wedding." Rachel stepped back, tugging her hair free from Harry's loose hold. "I'll marry you in eight years' time at the latest. That should give us time to finish whatever else Outward Bound wants to throw at us. That will also give me time to grow a metre and a half or so of hair — oh, crippen. It won't, will it?"

"No. You'll have about three years' worth of growth plus . . . um . . . two months or so." He tweaked her nose gently. "Better get growing. Want me to do it too?"

Rachel shook her head. "And have you taking all the glory? Doctor Fejoa, I want you to sport no more than . . . um . . . " She moved her finger and thumb close together and squinted at him through the gap. "About this much. And *no* beard. Scratchy."

"You've never said so on the islands or in the sim," he said, taken aback.

"You can't help it then. If you don't want to clip and shave, you can probably get a hair-retardant. Or tank your head."

Harry kissed her to stop the nonsense. He had no doubt it was tank euphoria talking, and he enjoyed it, but he had other things to think of than the speed of hair growth.

The euphoria held while they went to eat soup and more of the pea-protein patties in the facility dining room.

They were halfway through the soup, and Rachel was entertaining herself and Harry by identifying all the ingredients, when Jonty, Sofia and Field came in.

Harry waved them over. "We're going to visit Doctor Shah when we finish here. Want to come?"

Jonty's face lit up. "Yes! The foal will be out of the tank, and I want to check on the rat. Maybe Toodles will make a special appearance. That's if he's still tanked."

The other two nodded enthusiastically.

"I'm starving," Sofia said. "I calculate we went two hours without food . . . plus the fasting beforehand."

"What is it with all these numbers?" Harry asked plaintively. "Rachel's been calculating how much hair she can grow before our wedding."

Sofia grinned. "I'm so envious of you two!"

Rachel put down her spoon. "You could have a celebration or thanksgiving service if you wanted."

"Damn right," Sofia said. "We're going to have *something*. Just haven't figured out what."

"Did that polyamory law ever get off the ground?" Jonty asked hopefully.

They exchanged glances and shrugged. None of them had any information about the workings of the outside world.

"We're going to need a hell of a catchup," Sofia said.

Harry almost agreed but then he reflected—why bother? They were shipping out, and on Magellan Sixteen they would have their own laws. He saw no reason why polyamory shouldn't be perfectly acceptable in a new world, as long as all parties agreed.

Not that he wanted anyone but Rachel, he thought, but some people flourished in multi-partner relationships.

And some people don't do well with even one partner, he pondered sadly, recalling Flavia's disastrous marriage.

A cold shadow passed over him. He'd asked Flav to marry him. He'd never intended more than a companionable relationship whereby he'd have the legal right to support Flav and little Turq . . . but what if Flav had agreed?

Brrr. He shivered.

Rachel turned to gaze at him. "Harry?"

"Nothing. I just remembered I want to contact Cataleya Conti. But we'll go to see the Shahs first. By the way," he added, for the benefit of the other three, "Doctor Shah's wife is in a tank."

Explaining that fact lasted until they had finished eating and headed out to the animal tanks.

Shah was there, with his hand on the panel of Tank One.

"Hello—sorry we didn't get to see you when we came off the island," Harry said.

Shah smiled at them with a bit less than his usual joie de vivre. "I knew there was a tight schedule."

"I suppose Ned's out?" Rachel said cheerfully.

Harry didn't blame her. What *did* one say to a man whose chosen life companion was sleeping in a tank for an unforeseeable period?

He made a mental note to ask for some accelerated learning while he was at the facility. He needed to catch up with medical advances . . . though he'd necessarily fall behind again when they did the big five.

Shah's smile brightened. "Yes, and he's doing well. Want to meet him?"

Jonty nodded enthusiastically.

Shah gave a quick pat to the tank and led the way out to the paddock.

"Who do you have in Tank One?" Rachel asked.

"That's Piggle. He's a miniature pig we had brought in. He's twelve."

"That's older than most of your subjects, isn't it?" Jonty ventured.

"Yes. We've mostly gone for smaller and younger subjects for logistical reasons, and to give us a longer post-tank period for observation. Piggle is what you might call a multiple rescue. His original owners thought he'd stay small forever, but he weighs in at over a hundred kilos. He was passed on to another family, who couldn't keep him from escaping, then to a farm, but he didn't do well because he regards himself as a . . . not a person, but he's conditioned to want company and affection. After he came here, Willow looked after him for a year then—" He turned out his hands.

"Cue a fuss?" Sofia asked.

"Not really. She's grown up a lot—too quickly. She knew Neddy Boy was coming out and she sat with Piggle while he went off to Snoozeland. That's her term, by the way." He caught Harry's eye. "We elected to give him gentle short-term anaesthesia before we put him in the tank so he wouldn't feel abandoned. Fortunately, we were right in our supposition Neddy would remember Willow. I think he was maybe surprised that she was bigger, but she had half an apple, so he soon forgave her. See?"

They had reached the yard where a skewbald Shetland was kicking up his heels while older animals watched him indulgently. "He's been out for two months, and he's a textbook example of a colt of his subjective age and type. Willow's a bit disappointed she's going to be too tall to ride him, but Inge and I got her a riding pony—Kanga. That's the grey. He's tall enough to carry her into her teens and he won't be tanked except in exceptional circumstances."

He gestured towards the carrot bin. "Grab some treats—Neddy will come over and say hi."

They fed the ponies, a couple of cows, and goats.

"How's Rani?" Rachel asked.

"Back in the tank," Shah said. "We weaned her litter and gave her a couple of weeks of R-and-R, then tanked her again. We're hoping to get another litter when she comes out, but the timing will be close. She's the first rat we've tanked twice."

He scratched a cow behind the poll.

Silence fell.

Harry said, "I hope Inge has as good an experience with tanking as we have."

"So do I." Shah looked at his left hand, where Harry saw a wedding ring. "I'd planned to tank an animal or two which was ill, or not thriving, to see if that works but the gang here is too healthy. All we can do is hope a cure comes for Inge before too long. I promised to stay around for Willow until Inge is back, even if it means tanking the pair of us — that's a joke — but" — he shrugged — "it did cross my mind that having one available parent leaves Willow vulnerable."

"What measures did you take?" Harry asked. "You know we all have champions . . . advocates to make decisions for us if necessary."

"Obviously he knows," Jonty put in. "I think most of us chose him — right?" She smiled at Shah.

"Yes. And I'm obviously acting for Inge. So is Amber. Willow will also come online if she's emancipation age before Inge is back." He shrugged. "Cure-coasting is so much in its infancy we need far more regulations and plans. Inge's chip is inoperable, and her finances and affairs are in stasis. She deregistered for tax and jury duty and so on. We had to work out how to remove her from being my cosignatory and Willow's functioning parent without declaring her dead or divorced or incompetent. It's all such new territory.

"And we, in a way, are lucky. I have access to the tech and hardware, and we live close to the facility. We also had time to plan, time to prepare Willow and Inge could make up her mind one day and be tanked the next. It would be much worse for someone with no infrastructure and foreknowledge. A trauma case, for example." He ran both hands through his hair. "I don't know that I see cure-coasting catching on for the population at large. Too many complications."

Harry saw his point. He and the other viabilities weren't ill. They didn't have to work out logistics, just live in pleasant surroundings with congenial people with no real stressors . . . oh, and spend some blink-and-miss-it time in a tank. It was all organised for them.

Then there was shipping out — the great adventure —

Harry added one more item to his to-do list. Ask someone, maybe Cataleya Conti, for an update on progress on *Elysian Dawn*. He hoped they'd soon be given a tour of the ship or as much of it as was currently built.

Not that we'll be spending much time in her.

The thought made him want to laugh, but it seemed likely they'd be roused from the tanks months or at least weeks before the ship landed. If she landed. Something so huge might have to remain in orbit while the passengers ferried themselves down in smaller craft.

More and more questions came into his mind. No doubt there would be a full briefing with the viabilities and the settlers-elect, but he wanted to get his mental ducks in a row.

Shah said, "I see Amber approaching with a purposeful step. I assume she's coming to gather you for debriefing or medical tests or to measure your toenails or hair growth or something—" He broke off when the viabilities laughed. "What?"

"Hair growth!" Rachel spluttered. "Oh—" She went off into another fit of giggles.

Jonty put her hand on Shah's and gave him a pat. "Never mind, Doctor Shah. You had to be there."

Chapter Seventeen: And Then There Were—, 2237

Amber reached them and greeted everyone with a quick on-off smile. "Official debriefing and announcement," she said apologetically.

"Can't we have it here?" Jonty seemed inclined to stay with the animals.

"Sorry," Amber said. "The summons is from on high." She rolled her eyes, but something in her demeanour made Harry look at her twice. He liked Amber, but she seemed less animated and less positive than she had a year ago. He wondered if there was an element of survivor guilt. She had to feel it on some level, he thought, no matter how unreasonable it was.

If she asked his advice, which she wouldn't, he'd encourage her to be glad she had good health so she could provide support for her niece.

They stepped into the tanking facility, and on to the main hall where briefings usually happened.

Harry was surprised, and pleased, to see Cataleya Conti there along with Bao Woo and Bindilina Ash.

"I need to talk to her about contacting my cousin," he said to Rachel.

"Do you think she can help?"

"Doctor Darling seems to think so. I might ask for all of us—those who have outside advocates and heirs."

"Good plan. They're more likely to give in if we all agree." Rachel squeezed his arm. "There's no reason why we shouldn't visit them, really. We're not due to tank again for a while . . . are we?"

Harry shrugged. "I expect they'll want to monitor us for a while to make sure there are no ill effects."

"There haven't been so far," Rachel said. "No one has dropped out because of ill effects from the tanking—unless Til—" She broke off. "What he did seemed really out of character."

Harry nodded. "But it was months after the week in the tank." He remembered Amber Fordyce suggesting Til Lund was on shaky ground—had she offered to find a way for him to contact Genevieve? If so, had anything ever come of that? He said more certainly, "I think Til's problem was less about the tanking than it was about feeling a lack of self-determination and isolation. After Genevieve dropped out, he had no natural confidante, whereas the rest of us—"

"Of course! We've all paired up. Or tripled up. Steel walked when Abra said she was leaving, and Esme didn't stay long after Lolly left." Rachel squeezed his hand. "If you want to drop out—for whatever reason—*tell me.* I want to do this, but I want to be with you much more. Say the word and I'll walk. We can get married and forget all about adventures in the stars."

"It's a bargain," Harry said, squeezing back.

She looked startled.

Harry laughed. "No, no! I mean, I want to do this too—but you are the person I want to do it with—or anything, really. So it's a bargain. If either of us has a change of mind, we will inform the other immediately. There will be no second guessing, no recriminations, just us."

Someone cleared his throat, and Harry stopped gazing into Rachel's clear brown eyes and turned reluctantly for yet another briefing, debriefing, pep-talk or whatever was in store for the viability team.

Inevitably it was Chavez, with his scornful eyes peering over his conquistadorial nose, who stood on a dais. Harry wondered fancifully if the man often got distracted by seeing the bridge of his own nose with both eyes.

"Elites, welcome back from your month in the tank. To save time and uncertainty, we are sending you out of the complex in a week's time. You may then return to Brierly Island, where you will remain until we recall you for the final round of tanking. This is a five-year stretch. Because you will be out of touch for a considerable time, you may apply to visit your designated heirs while awaiting the final stage. If you wish to change your arrangements, you will have time to do so. You will be allocated funds for such travel or further education you wish to undertake.

"Your chips will be reactivated if and when you apply to take advantage of this offer. When you have done whatever you wish, if we haven't contacted you first, you may contact Outward Bound via your chip and we will convey you to Brierly Island, or to any of our facilities where you may work as a recruiter. Should you wish to take advantage of any of these offers, please see Bao Woo, who will make arrangements for you."

He paused, staring around at the group.

"Please use this time to put your lives in order, if you have not already done so, to carry out any activities you wish and to decide if you want to proceed to the final tanking test. Re-examine your commitment to the Outward Bound project. Thank you for your attention."

Chavez turned and left the room.

Rachel said, in a rather high voice, "Harry — what was all that about?"

"I don't know — but I wonder if it had to do with Til's meltdown. Maybe Chavez has realised keeping such a strangling grip on volunteers may not be in his best interests." Harry turned to see what the others thought.

Field looked baffled, as did Jonty and Sofia.

He glanced around to see what Martin and Cherry made of it but couldn't immediately see them.

Rachel must have been doing likewise, because she said, "Where's Cherry?"

"With Martin," Sofia said. "And before you ask, I don't know where he is. They must have slipped through Nurse Fordyce's net."

"They were never in it," Rachel said. "They didn't come with us to see Neddy. It was just Harry and me and you three."

"Are you sure?" Sofia turned in a circle. "All right. Did they eat before we came from the showers?"

"We didn't see them," Harry said. He thought of the time he and Rachel had taken in the shower. "Maybe they left before we came out."

"Left where?" Sofia asked.

Harry shook his head.

"They've got to be somewhere," Rachel said logically. "Has anyone seen them at all today?"

Heads shook.

Jonty said, "I was talking to Cherry yesterday." She broke off as the others stared at her. "What?"

"Last month," Rachel said.

"So it was. It goes by so quickly. Anyway, we were talking while we waited. We were all prepped, and Martin had already gone in—Cherry was saying he'd be in before her and so out before her, and maybe he'd do the sleeping beauty kiss ... yes, I know, we were talking rubbish, but you know how it is. All the waiting around means you babble whatever's in your head." She turned to Harry. "I suppose you didn't see Martin?"

"No, I'm the first one under," Harry said. "Then it's

Martin, as you said, then you, Sofia, and Jonty, Field, Rachel, and Cherry."

"That sounds right. I went into my tank cubicle. I didn't say anything more to Cherry because I knew I'd see her again in an hour or so. So to speak."

They were still pondering the whereabouts of their missing teammates when Amber Fordyce came over to them. She still looked strained.

"I might as well tell you, Martin Fong and Cherry York have left the program," she said.

They gaped at her.

Harry said, "Do you know why, Amber?"

"Not officially."

"Unofficially."

"Do you all feel well?" she asked abruptly.

"Great—as usual," Rachel said.

The others nodded.

"We always do feel well after tanking," Jonty added.

"Well—Cherry didn't do as well in the post-tank tests as expected." Amber held up her hand. "She's fine. She was just a bit disoriented. Doctor Darling thinks it's the dislocation effect of waking up a month later than one's body thinks it is—something like waking in the morning and discovering it's almost dinner time or dreaming a long journey and waking to discover you haven't left home yet. Anyway, Cherry has left the facility. She's gone to one of the other campuses for a rest, and Martin elected to go with her."

"When are they coming back?" Jonty asked.

"I don't know if they are, either officially or unofficially. However, I do advise you to keep a close eye on yourselves and one another for the next few days. If you notice any disorientation or headaches, dizziness, déjà vu, double vision, depression, anxiety, nausea—"

"Whoa!" Field said, holding up his hand. "We'll report any

physical, mental or emotional problems to you or the doctor. How's that?"

"But we don't have any," Rachel protested. "If it makes you all feel better, we'll stay here for the week ... maybe help Doctor Shah with the animals... but according to Chavez, we can also go out—out into the world, I mean."

"Was that your suggestion?" Harry asked the nurse. "I was talking to you about contacting my cousin."

Amber lifted a shoulder. "I may have mentioned something to Doctor Darling. I don't know where it went from there, but if you want to make arrangements I suggest you catch up with the board members right now." She indicated Cataleya Conti, who was in conversation with Woo and Ash.

"Just don't go anywhere for at least a week, and report immediately if you feel any ill effects. It's vital for your welfare *and* for the future of the project ... not to speak of my sister and others like her."

She gave them a nervous smile and scurried away.

Rachel raised her eyebrows, hands and shoulders and pulled a wry face. "And then there were five."

CHAPTER EIGHTEEN: OUT IN THE WORLD, 2237-38

Harry and Rachel stayed for the required week then, with their chips reactivated and travel reservations and funds provided by Bao Woo, they travelled in the familiar truck to the nearest zip.

It was five years since they'd been out of the project territory, and it felt bizarre. Harry had decided to top up his medical qualifications, and Rachel wanted to learn more about making textiles from natural fibres, both vegetable and animal in nature. They found a facility that would allow them both to study, but before they moved into the accommodation provided, Harry took Rachel to his old riverside apartment to introduce her to Flavia and Harley.

"Turq was three when I last saw her, so she'll be eight or so now," he said as they shared a zip cabin on the fast line.

"Why do you call her Turq?"

Harry smiled. "She always wears turquoise clothing. Last time I saw her, she had an oversized shirt on. She's so funny about it! Blue won't do, purple is out of the question, and as for green! She's not even happy about aqua or teal! Luckily Flav got hold of a big pack of *Re-dye-it* in the grub's favourite shade."

"You do know she might have grown out of that obsession," Rachel said gently.

Harry did know, objectively. However, his mind refused to accept Harley Neal as anything but a sticky urchin wearing oversized garments in that striking colour.

"I take it her father isn't in the picture," Rachel added.

"No. That is, I never met him, and I don't know much about him. Flavia looked out for me after my parents died. She couldn't adopt me, because we were deemed too close in age, but she was my guardian. That turned out to be fortunate in one way. I got into medical school young under the Emancipated Orphans' Grant—remember that?"

She nodded. "I couldn't use it because my parents were still alive. Some technicality." Her expression turned a bit dark. "I have a feeling *they* had pay-offs from the white coat institute who'd undertaken to make me ... conformable ... and failed."

Harry winced in sympathy. "Are they still alive now? As in, were they when you first went to Outward Bound?" He wouldn't mind paying them a visit.

Rachel's eyes hardened. "I don't know. I haven't seen them or heard from them since they handed me over to the white coats on a long lease."

"Then I assume you don't feel any obligation to tell them your plans."

"None whatsoever." Her eyes returned to their warm brown. "Harry, *you* are my family. You're my today and my tomorrows—all of them."

"All good then," he said. If this was Rachel's way of dealing with past betrayals, well and fine. He resolved, consciously and finally, that she'd never be betrayed again. Not on his watch.

Rachel smiled. "Indeed. Go on."

Go on ... oh! He continued his narrative. "I took the accelerated learning option because I wasn't sure how the funds would hold out once I reached full emancipation age. I didn't see much of Flav during that time ... I was too busy and had nothing to spare for travel. I worked as a tutor to some students older than I was and threw everything I could earn into completing my last year of accelerated training. When Flav and I caught up again, I invited her to my graduation. She came—and when I took her home I found out she had a baby. The woman in the next apartment had looked after Turq for a few hours so Flav could go out.

"Flav didn't tell me much, but she was living in a fairly dire place. I found out eventually she was pretty much in hiding.

"I couldn't help her out—then—but I passed on my apartment when I joined Outward Bound. I'd have had them to live with me before, but I had a single adult's room until I started work with the company."

"And they're still there."

"As far as I know. The apartment is designated for one adult, but Flav and Turq can live there until the grub ages out. After that—" He sighed. "I suggested they apply to ship out, but Flav said she was too old. I'm hoping to change her mind on that."

"Is there any age requirement?" Rachel asked. "I don't remember anything being said."

"Not that I've heard, either." He realised he knew very little about the requirements for the settlers elect.

"It would make sense to send a broad range of ages and types to mimic family structure," Rachel said.

"Yes—but can you imagine someone middle-aged wanting to cut ties with Terra forever?"

"We'll be middle-aged by the time we ship out."

"Barely, and we're used to the idea. And we don't have strong ties except with one another."

"You have your cousins."

"Yes, but they're better off if I go . . . I can pass on the payments and set them up for life. Flav deserves something nice—she's one of the best people I know." He paused, remembering. "I was twelve when my parents died. Flav was twenty-seven. She and I had met *once . . .* and yet she was the one who came for me. She wouldn't touch a credit of the Dependent grant and she helped me to apply for the Emancie funds. I owe her so much, and leaving Terra is the best way to repay that."

"We have ties with the other viabilities," Rachel ventured.

"Well, yes, but how many of them are still planning to ship out?"

"I suppose . . . " Rachel frowned. "I hope your cousin likes me."

"She will. And Turq will love you. Offer her cheese."

"You make her sound like a pet."

He laughed at her reproving tone. "She's a great little grub. Happiest kid I ever saw."

Rachel stretched, disengaging from the subject. "It feels so weird to be wearing something other than island clothes or paper gowns."

It did. Harry had been surprised, but relieved, when Conti came to the facility three days after the de-tanking with a bag of clothing for them both. They already had the travel packs from Woo, but the clothes in those were the utilitarian garments of the style they'd had in the sim. He looked Rachel over. Conti's own clothing sense tended to be plain and matronly, but she'd brought soft brown pants with a lighter top for Rachel.

"Cornelia suggested this would be acceptable," she'd said as if in explanation. "My niece," she'd clarified as an afterthought. "She's sixteen."

The colour exactly echoed Rachel's brown eyes. The neckline of the top was trimmed with a narrow gold satin braid. Her hair, still silky and soft from whichever of the tanking liquids was responsible for the effect, was tied back in a tail.

Harry thought of her desire to out-Rapunzel Rapunzel at their wedding. That was still some time in their future, but they *were* moving on.

One tanking to go. And we're outside – out in the world.

The notion felt surreal, and he suspected he and Rachel had already mentally divorced themselves from their Terran lives.

He hoped their studies would have more reality. If they didn't *believe* the studies were relevant, then they wouldn't stick.

"When we get to work at the learning facility next week, I wonder if Outward Bound will feel real to us," he said.

"I doubt it." Rachel squeezed his hand. "But *we're* real. You and me. Our family."

"Oh, *we're* real." He had no doubts about that.

He remembered Cherry York's concerns about what had happened to the viabilities who had left. He hoped those concerns had all been allayed for her now.

He and Rachel hadn't cashed out, but they'd been given quite enough to keep them comfortable for the next several months. He might have thought *for the next several years,* but prices had risen a lot. The government's *eat to live* policy meant it was technically possible to survive on the state food allowance. No one would starve on the basic rations, but prices had shot up for everything *but* the most basic food. Most food also seemed blander than he remembered.

Zip travel was less streamlined than it had been. Robot porters checked the carriages at every stop.

Harry and Rachel were required to touch their chips to every door.

"I'd forgotten how much faffing about there is outside," Rachel said. She added, "Is there more than there used to be? Or is it my imagination? Has Outward Bound tamed us?"

"Definitely not your imagination, and *no one* could tame you."

"The white coats tried."

"And failed magnificently," he said cordially. "I ought to congratulate them."

News bulletins flashed on walls as they travelled.

Harry didn't activate the sound links, which would have cost more than the trip itself, but none of it looked good.

When the zip carriage stopped, they had to touch their chips to the panel again. The door wouldn't open. Print sprawled across the panel.

Imprint destination and purpose of visit.

Harry didn't like this. It was no one's business but their own if they visited his old apartment.

Counting ducks by the river, he typed.

"Harry!" Rachel sounded shocked and amused.

"Well, we will!"

The door opened.

The zip clicked and the carriage continued around the circuit.

"How far is it to your apartment?" Rachel asked.

"About ten minutes' walk." He supposed it was his apartment, technically. It was registered to him, although Flav was the current tenant.

"Lovely." Rachel beamed with what looked to be real pleasure.

They left the platform and took the path to the river.

"This used to be grass," Harry said, frowning at the smooth rubbery coating underfoot.

"I suppose we knew tech would keep on being invented while we were away." Rachel indicated the waterway ahead. "That looks very . . . clean."

It did look clean—abnormally, unnaturally clean. Harry consulted his memory of the brown meandering river bobbing with ducks and krakens of water weed. It had been clean. Mud and logs were as much a part of its ecology as the uptailed ducks.

Now—

It might as well be a sanitised gutter, he thought. They wouldn't be counting ducks after all.

He felt a sense of personal ill-usage. This had been his quiet place when he was first working for Outward Bound.

They took the path along the bank until they reached the branch track that led to his apartment among the trees.

"There it is." He indicated the square unit with the white-painted door.

It looked a bit grubby, but he supposed that was inevitable with Harley Neal racing in and out, opening and closing the panel with whatever stickiness she retained as she outgrew toddlerhood.

He supposed his chip would still open the door, unless copying it over to Flav had automatically cancelled it for his own use.

He tapped softly, just in case.

He even had his opening salvo waiting: *Hope you're prepared to butter us a bun.*

The door banged open so suddenly he and Rachel stumbled back.

A middle-aged man with blond hair and eyelashes stood on the threshold, staring at them with pale blue eyes. "Yes?"

Rachel said, "Hello. We're looking for Williams Lund. Do we have the right place?"

"No." He smiled. "Sorry."

"Oh. Do you happen to know where he is?"

"Never heard of him."

Rachel glanced at Harry. "Bother. He must have moved. How annoying. I thought he said he'd be here when we got back." She returned her attention to the man, who was still smiling. "Do you live here, Mister —"

He nodded but ignored the invitation to give her his name.

"Have you been here long?"

"Long enough. This is my wife's place. I'm waiting for her to come home." His smile dimmed. "How long ago are we talking, here? There was a guy living here before she and our kid moved in, but his name wasn't William Tun."

"Williams Lund," Rachel corrected. "And it would be . . . " She glanced at Harry again. "How long, Bram?"

He shrugged. "Six . . . maybe seven years back."

"Before our time. But if you give me your names, I can ask my wife when she arrives."

"Sure. Bram and Delia Duckworthy," Rachel said glibly. She spelled the names. "You can contact us at Facility Nine, extension seven-seven-eighty-nine. Want me to write it down?"

He shook his head, then tapped his temple. "I never forget."

"Trick memory, eh? I knew a woman like that, once. Nina Beach. Are you related?"

He shook his head.

"Right, come on Bram." Rachel took Harry's hand and turned away from the door. As they walked back down the track, she said, "That's so odd. I'm *sure* Willie said it was this place he was moving to. Are there any other riverside apartments, I wonder?"

"Bound to be," Harry said. "We ought to have checked with Joelson before we came all the way out here. Back to square one, eh, Dee-Dee?"

They walked on, not looking back.

Finally, Harry said, "I'm supposing that charade was for a reason?"

"Yes. He's—there's something wrong with him."

"Clearsight tell you that?"

"Hm. He's been a red-chip."

"Oh."

Something stirred in Harry's memory.

"Flav's husband was a red-chip."

"The one you never met."

"Yes. Damn. I suppose this means he found her. Rach, was there anyone else there?"

140

"No. Just him." She shivered. "I'm glad you didn't try to open the door."

Harry said, "I wonder what would have happened if I'd said I was looking for Flavia and Harley Neal?"

"I don't know, but I think we—and they—are safer not finding out."

"*Damn*," Harry said. "I thought they'd be safe there. Should have known better."

"How could you have known?"

"The place they lived before, Pleasant View Apartments, is a rat-warren . . . and nothing like so nice as the one Doctor Shah had Rani in. Flav said people often left without warning. It was so crowded no one would have been able to locate one woman and child there. At the riverside apartment it would have been too easy . . . one woman with a child in a single-adult apartment. And he might have known who I was."

Rachel put her arm around him. "None of this is your fault, but Harry—I don't think we should look for your cousins. I just hope they got away safely. I think we'd better get somewhere safe too—and stay there."

"That's what we'll do. Rach, how did you know not to give Flav's name or ours?"

"There was something off about him . . . and you'd said they lived there alone. He said—implied—they were going to be there together. I suppose you can't have him evicted?"

"I doubt it. He must have been re-chipped, so technically he's not doing anything illegal."

They returned to the academy and moved into the supported accommodation—in their case, one of eight hundred identical apartments. Harry, with five years of medical updates to learn, settled into a regimen of accelerated study.

He was grateful to his brain that this was possible. Some people couldn't use the augmented download system. It confused their minds, and top-loading knowledge sometimes displaced things they'd learned earlier. Harry had never had trouble like that. After five years away, he picked up benchmarks and levels at a speed that surprised even him.

Rachel, who preferred a slower form of study, insisted on taking at least two free days a week for rest and recreation.

"You still knit," he pointed out.

"So do you. Anyway, that's relaxing. Harry, when we ship out you won't be able to use the accelerated study."

"No. But by then, I hope I'll know enough to extrapolate the things I need to learn. Once we're on Magellan Sixteen, there will be a whole new field of study which we'll have to do the old-fashioned way by observation and reasoning."

"Applying everything we know to a new environment. Are xenodiseases actually likely to attack us, do you think?"

"I don't know. Insufficient data. But if our crops grow easily we'll have to be wary, because that will signify Terran life is comfortable on Magellan Sixteen."

"And if they don't grow easily, we'll be in trouble anyway. Harry, are we mad to even consider this?"

"Undoubtedly," he said. "But the signs are that the atmosphere and temperature are Terra-like, and minerals seem to be the same everywhere they're sampled."

"Q.E.D., our crops *will* grow, and we'll just have to hope the local diseases put us in the too-hard basket."

"Yes." He put his arms around her and tugged at the tail of hair that now stretched past her shoulder blades. "What's brought this on, Rach?"

She kissed his neck. "I'm not sure. Maybe the tanking euphoria is wearing off. Maybe it's claustrophobia. This place is tiny."

"Bigger than a tank."

"Yes, but—Harry, I know what I'd like to do."

"What's that?"

"I want a trip to my glorious emptiness."

"You haven't got a headache, have you?"

She pulled back. "Of course not! The only time I ever had those was in the blasted sim. I just love the wide space and the stars and the openness of it all. It accepts me. It expects nothing. Will you?"

"Of course I will. Put your knitting down."

"Why? I might knit the mist and spangle it with stars just for you." She batted her eyelashes at him.

Harry laughed.

"Hmph!" Rachel put aside her knitting and let herself down on the bed that occupied a quarter of their floorspace. She folded one arm across her stomach and held out her other hand invitingly.

Harry lay down beside her, holding her hand.

"Close your eyes."

"Way ahead of you!"

"You're moving gently out of the daylight into a vast . . . " Her hand slackened. He let his voice settle into silence.

Flav and Turq — hope you're okay. Hope I didn't bring you to harm.

CHAPTER NINETEEN: ELYSIAN DAWN, EARLY 2239

When Bao Woo of Outward Bound came to visit them in their room, Harry assumed it was time to report for their five-year tanking. He was already mentally cataloguing the preparations they'd need to make when Woo made his small habitual bow and smiled.

Woo was, Harry supposed, about fifty years old. It was hard to tell. It was also difficult with Landon Chavez, whose harsh features almost certainly made him look older than he was, but Woo had regular features and a smooth brow. His black hair was not yet greying.

Rachel was greeting him with a friendly hello and Harry waited expectantly.

Woo looked from Rachel to Harry and back again. "I trust you're well?"

"Perfectly," Rachel said. "You? And your wife and daughter?"

He nodded. "Indeed. Zan—or Samantha as she now chooses to be called—is in college, and Hui Fen sends greetings."

"Please send ours back to her," Rachel said. It was a ritual, although they had never met Woo's family.

Woo said, "I have come with an invitation for you to visit *Elysian Dawn*." He held up his hand. "She is not yet habitable, but her skeletal frame is now complete. This involves a short shuttle trip to her orbit, where we intend to document the landmark of progress, but we—the board—felt our elites would enjoy a chance to see her."

"When?" Rachel blurted.

"Today," Woo said placidly. "There will be room in the shuttle. Do you wish to come?"

"We do." Harry had intended to check with Conti about the ship's status but hadn't found the opportunity.

"Very good." Woo indicated the door. "The carrier is waiting."

Hurry up and wait, Harry thought ironically as they followed Woo to the truck. He could tell Rachel was excited by the tiny skip in her step.

Her enthusiasm for life was infectious. She always embraced opportunity . . . and him . . . head-on. He thought that might tell him something about himself if he stopped to self-analyse.

"Onwards and upwards," he whispered, lifting her into the back of the truck, just because he could.

"Outward bound," she whispered back, before kissing him.

"Always."

The sound of applause made them break apart, laughing, to greet Field, Jonty and Sofia who were already seated in the vehicle.

Rachel went to hug all three.

Harry didn't ask if they were still together because it was obvious they were from the way Field sat in the middle with an arm around each woman. Instead, he and Rachel sat on the facing seats.

"So, what have you been doing?" Jonty and Rachel burst out together.

"Jinx!" they chorused.

Rachel said, "I'm studying fabrics and design . . . not just clothing but lightweight fibres that might work for temporary shelters at Journey's End."

They had taken to calling Magellan Sixteen that. As Rachel said, it did save two syllables and it did mark the completion of their tanking journey.

"That must depend on the native fibres," Sofia put in.

"We'll take bamboo and maybe pandanus with us."

Jonty said, "I've been studying too — practical studies in husbandry."

The catchup lasted them for some time, during which Harry realized he hadn't asked where they were going or for how long.

Woo's urbane friendliness had disarmed them all, he thought. They were all curious, intelligent people, but they had been conditioned to accept whatever Outward Bound decided to do . . . other than Til Lund's abrupt blow-up and exit from the program, he could barely remember any challenge other than his own in the matter of funds, of being anaesthetised without warning and being kept in hospital. His challenges in these matters had been accepted with good grace, so why had there been so few . . .

Ah, that's why! he thought, suddenly enlightened. People who think they have a good chance of getting what they want are probably more likely to trust their masters.

And this unexpected treat . . . was it a carrot for cooperative donkeys? Or did the Outward Bound folk think visiting their future home-in-the-stars would kick-start any waning enthusiasm?

He didn't bother to voice any of these matters because whether or not his conclusions were fact it didn't matter. The results would be the same.

With just five of them in a vehicle that could have carried twenty, there was plenty of room, and they slept and ate when the mood took them.

They were asleep when they reached their destination and,

woken, advised to a toilet break, then ushered across a mostly dark space-field with little time to speculate.

The shuttle was shaped like a truncated pencil, with strap-in seats around the walls.

"It's going to take them forever to get everyone to the ship if they use this," Sofia said as she buckled herself in.

A technician they didn't know walked around checking everyone's straps before Woo, Chavez and two others of the board entered and took their places.

"No waivers?" Field asked.

"Your general waivers are still in force," Chavez said.

"No health checks and questionnaires?" Jonty added.

"You've all been monitored and passed fit for tanking," one of the strangers said.

The tech, who turned out to be the pilot as well, gave them a short pre-flight lecture suggesting they might find acceleration uncomfortable and should stay strapped in until or unless advised.

Harry relaxed into his seat. The thing was slung on gimbals, which would allow it to assume different positions. He concentrated on breathing steadily.

Acceleration was definitely uncomfortable, as were the pressure suits they wore, but when they reached their destination Harry knew it was worth the trip.

They came upon her suddenly, rather than seeing her looming in from far off.

Elysian Dawn was vast. He had seen the ship's blueprint and an artist's impression and regretted its lack of refined beauty, but seeing its framework bolted to an enormous platform floating in orbit made an impression he knew he'd remember for the rest of his life. The ship was so big the curving skeleton seemed infinite, as if he hung suspended in a hall of mirrors.

"It's glorious," Rachel said. She lifted one hand, slowly,

because the pressure suit controlled her movements. "Look, Harry, *that's* where our tank's going to be."

Harry knew she was playing games . . . or was she? With her hyper focus, perhaps she could see more detail and not be distracted by immensity and the lack of perspective and scale.

The shuttle had matched orbits with the behemoth, smaller than a cleaner wrasse in comparison with a whale. Three of the passengers unstrapped themselves and became busy with equipment, which Harry realised was making a three-dimensional scan which appeared on a monitor.

He switched his gaze between the real-time view and the growing impression, where points of light spread out translucent wings to build a virtual ship.

Then he glanced at Rachel and saw her rapt expression. He realised with a jolt that she was looking away, over and past the ship, into the vast emptiness of entrancement.

With an effort, he unstrapped and floated over to her, gripping her seat and looking into her eyes.

"Where are you, Rachel?" he asked softly.

"Outward bound," she replied in a whisper.

The captain, if that was what he was, turned ponderously from the equipment he was operating and frowned at Harry.

"Doctor Fejoa, please return to your seat."

Harry hovered where he was, but Rachel turned and smiled at him. "Are you supposed to be here?"

That echo of what he had said to her in the shower after the six-day tanking made him smile, and after a moment he nodded to the captain and returned to his seat.

The man checked his clips and buckles, and Harry suspected he would find it far more difficult to leave his seat a second time. Wisely, he didn't try.

When the virtual simulation of the ship was done, the shuttle left its matched orbit and began the long curve to match instead with its landing pad.

Once landed, and with the five viabilities quickly assessed and debriefed, they returned to the truck and were taken back to their pick-up points.

"Isn't she glorious?" Rachel said dreamily as they got into bed in their cramped accommodation.

"Impressive," Harry allowed. "What did you see when you were watching the framework?"

Rachel said, "It was fractals, but I think those were something from my mind. It's going to be perfectly ordinary inside, surely."

"We'll be tanked most of the time," Harry reminded.

"Ye-es, but there has to be storage for animal tanks, and all the ground-breaking future proofing equipment . . . having everything low-tech means more storage room. Harry — will you miss tech?"

"I doubt if we'll have time," he said.

"No." Unexpectedly, Rachel laughed.

"Now what?"

"I just thought of Doctor Shah. He's probably in charge of supplying the animals for Journey's End. I wonder if he'll stow away to make sure they're properly cared for at the other end."

"If he doesn't, he'll want them to send postcards from *Elysian Dawn*," Harry said.

Rachel poked him. "Harry, you say the most peculiar things."

CHAPTER TWENTY: CLOAKS, 2239-40

Harry wondered what other field trips or enticements might be on offer, but their venture into the building zone was the first and last. After a while, he gave up expecting an invitation and focused on his studies and on Rachel.

They had just about exhausted the studies they could do when they were summoned, not for a joyride into space, but back to Outward Bound.

Their hiatus out in the world was over.

Used to uncertain timelines, they disposed of most of their few portable belongings and relinquished their apartment.

"Won't miss that," Rachel stated as they closed the door and used their chips to sign out for the last time. "Wonder if we get the rest of the week's utility funds back?"

"We ought to," Harry said. "They'll have someone back in here in ten, nine, eight . . ."

Rachel giggled, indicating a young Asian woman climbing the other curve of the stairs. "And here she is."

The girl glanced at them, did a classic doubletake, and looked again.

"Hello?" Harry said.

"Hi." She looked again. "Great cloaks . . . or are they blankets?"

"Cloaks," Rachel said, handing one to Harry. "We've been knitting for a couple of years, and I sewed it all together in patchwork."

"Shiny," the girl said. She indicated her high-collared red brocade blouse. "I like colour."

"Me too," Rachel said.

"I'm Samantha." She gave them another stare from under a sharply cut black fringe. Her hair came down in geometric precision to her high cheekbones. "Are you Doctor Fejoa and Ms Traveller?"

"Yes," Harry said. He glanced at Rachel, but she was half-smiling. Evidently she sensed nothing *wrong* with this young woman.

"Thought you might be. My dad described you, He didn't mention the cloaks, though." She gave them a nod and set herself back in motion up the stair.

Harry and Rachel continued down.

"I take it *that* was Bao Woo's daughter," Harry said after a dozen steps.

"Small world," Rachel said. "Put your cloak on. Save carrying it."

Harry had never seen himself as a cloak person, but he complied, finding his new garment surprisingly light and warm.

"Observe—it has a hood," Rachel said happily. She swung her own cloak over her shoulders and did up the buttons that held it in place.

"I hope we don't get brought in as suspiciously cultish characters," Harry said, peering out from his hood, which stood out a good hands-breadth beyond his nose. "Watch your step. If you tread on your hem . . ."

"They'll do nicely on Journey's End. Probably be the new fashion," Rachel said.

Harry turned to look at her. Her face was straight, and he realised he had no idea whether she really intended to take the garments along. He supposed it might be possible. They would have to wear something after they emerged from the tanks, and wool was an adaptable fabric.

"That reminds me," he said, following his train of thought

as they rounded another curve and began on a new flight.

"What? About how fashion-forward we might be in our new world?"

"No — the tanks. Do you have any memory at all of coming out of one? We've been tanked three times now."

She shook her head and shrugged. "I always wake up wrapped in a towel . . . oh, I see what you mean. We climb in by ourselves, but someone must be taking us out."

"Or else we're climbing out by ourselves and just don't remember. Either way, there'll be no one to take us out or wrap us in towels when we reach Journey's End."

"Very true. But I'm sure they've thought of that," Rachel said comfortably. "Maybe they'll set the tanks to auto-drain, and we'll wake up — bump — on the bottom." She added, "I wonder if Inge Shah is out yet."

Harry consulted his new knowledge from the intensive study program. With so much information to absorb, he had automatically packed it into a mental index system, with watchwords. "I don't think that particular breakthrough has been made yet," he said regretfully.

Rachel sighed. "Let's hope something happens for her in the next five years. I'd love to have Inge at our wedding."

They had planned to be married in 2242, now two years away, but that was when they'd expected the *big five* tanking to follow much closer to the month-long session. The new plan was to make the date for two months after they left the tank. Surely, as Rachel had put it, that would have given Outward Bound sufficient time to sort out debriefing.

We're doing it . . . even if we have to import a celebrant to Honeymoon Island or wherever else they might decide to store us. Even if Field or Jonty or Sofia has to do an accelerated course in marrying.

Maybe Chavez will do it, he'd suggested, just for the fun of seeing her face.

I will not be married by Chavez!

"Are we going to wear these for the wedding?" Harry,

grinning privately at his memory flashes, swished his cloak as they reached the ground floor.

"No. At least, *you* may, but *I* want something slinky and pale. Rapunzel, remember."

Harry's grin broadened at the mind picture that conjured. "There's an old binding ceremony that had the couple's hands bound with a ribbon or silk cord. We might use your hair."

"It's a date though?" Rachel paused and looked at him with an expression he could describe only as adoring.

It was amazing to be adored. Even more amazing was the knowledge that he deserved it for the very reason of his own adoration of her.

They reached the outer door of the complex and signed themselves out. At that point they had to stop talking non-sense while they hurried to catch the zip.

"They might have brought the truck," Rachel grumbled.

The trip was even slower than their outward journey had been, with even more stops and automatic intrusions.

They arrived at the Outward Bound offices — the ones they had initially visited — where they were greeted by Cataleya Conti.

"Ready?" she asked, gazing in apparent wonder at their cloaks.

"Are we going straight to the tanks?" Rachel asked brightly.

"More or less. Why?"

"The sooner we're tanked, the sooner we're untanked, and the sooner we can start organising our wedding. You're invited, by the way. Bring your lovely niece who helped pick my clothes. Carnelian . . . Cordelia . . ."

Conti said, "Cornelia. It's a bit of a *thing* in our family to use the CC initials . . . I can introduce you, if you like. She's just joined Outward Bound."

"We met Samantha Woo as we were leaving this morning,"

Rachel said. "Do she and Cornelia know one another?"

Conti said, "Who knows? Not officially, if that's what you meant. When did you last eat?"

"Breakfast this morning," Rachel said. "We had it in bed." Her tone gave Harry another memory flash that had him grinning like a . . . well, his face felt stretched to the max.

Conti looked enquiring, and he said hastily, "That was twelve hours ago."

"Then you can probably be tanked tonight."

"Are the others coming? Sofia, Field and Jonty?"

"Bound to be," Rachel put in. "They came on the space jaunt." She glanced at Conti. "Have you been out to see *Elysian Dawn*?"

"No. And that's by choice. I like to stay on the ground. As for your colleagues—" Conti shrugged. "I was asked to fetch you two." She indicated a lightweight vehicle. "Jump in the back. We'll be there by sunset."

"What happened to the one-way-window truck?" Rachel whispered as she settled next to Harry.

Conti must have had good hearing, because she said, "We've had to stop using it when your numbers dropped. It contravenes the new size-per-passenger law." She sighed.

"When did that come in?" Harry asked.

"After our space jaunt," Rachel reminded him.

Conti's answer was inaudible as a large crack of thunder snapped overhead.

Chapter Twenty-One: See You in the Morning, October 2240

The storm was over by the time they reached the tank facility, but water streamed across the road and dashed along the gutters.

Conti let Harry and Rachel out of the vehicle and led them into the facility.

Chavez was there with well over a dozen others from the board, including Woo and Ash. With them stood Doctor Darling and, surprisingly, Doctor Shah. There were also well-dressed people who were probably investors and a sprinkling of younger people in their late teens or early twenties. Presumably one of them was Conti's niece.

Harry sighed. He wasn't in the mood for yet another debriefing and another long round of pointless questions. He looked round covertly, holding Rachel's hand and hoping to see Amber Fordyce. He had questions for her, and he'd like some answers before he stepped back into a tank.

Not that he could do anything about the answers today, he admitted to himself. Tomorrow? His tomorrow was five years in the future.

Chavez greeted the gathering and ran through the achievements and advances of Outward Bound so far.

Harry slid into a light trance and half-listened to the information that the FeTtL drive was in its late testing phase.

Isn't that what they said five years ago?

The final tank tests were underway, and the nominations

for colonists-elect were on a temporary hiatus.

Harry came alert at the sudden jerk of Rachel's hand in his.

"Why is that?" a man in a turban asked.

Chavez said, "You are?" in an oddly accusing tone.

"Doctor Dinesh Sheth of the Ganges Foundation, New Delhi," the man supplied.

Harry frowned, trying to access his faint memory of that name.

"He's one of the developers of FeTtL drive," Rachel murmured.

"Ah!" That made sense, he supposed.

Chavez said, "You should apply to Doctor Francesca Arblette for the answer to that question."

Doctor Sheth said, mildly, "If you tell me how to contact her, I will do so."

A woman whom Harry could not remember seeing before raised a hand above her head and pushed over to the dais. "I am Francesca Arblette. And the answer to Doctor Sheth's question is obvious." She paused, looking around with an odd expression on her round, dimpled face.

Harry thought she looked smug. Or maybe triumphant was the better term.

No one responded, so she launched into a fluent spiel.

"Not to negate the sterling work done by the recruiting team over the past few years" — she glanced around the board-members — "but it has been decided that a long lead-time is not in the best interests of the Outward Bound company or of the colonists-elect.

"Choosing from the pool of current applicants — though I understand these people have been carefully vetted and selected — would be feasible if Launch could be expected in twenty-two forty-one, or even forty-two. As it is, you can't possibly launch before twenty-two fifty-three at the very earliest — "

"We are committed to that date," Chavez broke in harshly.

"Very well, but, clearly, that is predicated on there being no further technological developments." She turned and raised her brows at Sheth, who looked enigmatically back. She cast her enquiring gaze around the group, smiling. "I'm sure you all understand this predicament."

No one said anything, so she continued. "Colonists-elect might seem perfect this year, but in thirteen years — or possibly fifteen — will they still be in the same glowing physical health? Today's forty-year-olds are tomorrow's fifty-fives, and their children, dependent minors of nine or ten now, who may be excited at the idea of living on a new world, will be adults in their mid-twenties with their own opinions and concerns." She slapped one fist into her other palm with a smack for emphasis. "The days of children being committed to some course of action their caregivers might choose have been — rightly — consigned to the past. After all, child marriage died out over a century ago. Young people of today are never encouraged, or allowed to make irrevocable decisions until — "

Rachel said, loudly and unexpectedly, "Tell that to Lolly Paringo!"

Doctor Arblette flung up her hands in slow motion and turned to smile at Rachel. "I don't believe I know that name . . . or yours."

"Lolly Paringo was an acrobat with the Cirque du Sud . . . she made the decision to train from a young age. Had she waited *until,* as you put it, she would have been too old, physically, to achieve her goals."

"Then it is as well such practices are no longer lawful," Arblette said.

"Ouch," Rachel muttered.

Harry agreed. He had wondered what happened to Lolly after she left the viability program. He'd thought she might have returned to train acrobats at Cirque du Sud, but if that had been disallowed, what could she be doing? He hoped her payout had been sufficient to give her some options.

There was a low murmur, and a board member said, "Doctor Arblette, you are suggesting that colonists need to be young, emancipated adults at the time of launch?"

"It seems sensible."

"Are you overlooking the wisdom and knowledge of mature citizens?" Bao Woo asked mildly with his habitual tiny bow.

"Not at all—yet you must admit such wisdom and knowledge comes at the price of a great deal of . . . " She hesitated, still smiling. "Dare I say *historical baggage? Outmoded notions?*"

A few people laughed uncertainly.

"There is also the possibility that older people might not be optimum candidates for stas-tanking. The truth is, no one over thirty has yet been successfully tanked, right?" She looked to Doctor Darling.

Before he could answer, if he had planned to, she added smoothly, "I made some enquiries and have learned that animal tests, which predate human tests by some years, have provided support for this theory." She indicated Doctor Shah. "Doctor, I believe your first experiments included"—she flicked out a handheld data screen and consulted it—"one mare, two sheep, and two goats, three of which died, yielding a sixty percent mortality rate. Hardly stellar."

Shah said, "No."

"No? You agree with me."

"No, I mean, that's not correct. Our first subjects were a common toad—*bufo bufo*—and three rats." He added, "Toodles, the toad and Rani, one of the rats, are still alive and well."

"Implying the others are not?" she said swiftly.

"It's true that Tatty and Parsnip died some time ago."

"As a result of being tanked."

Shah laughed. "On the contrary, their deaths came as a result of *not* being tanked — or to be precise, re-tanked. They were given short spells in the tank. After extraction, they lived perfectly normal and very healthy rat lifespans until they died of natural causes." He added, gently, "Rats rarely live to be four years old, although toads might make it to ten or even to twelve. Putting it that way, you might say our first experiments concluded with a hundred percent success rate."

"I see. I was informed —"

Shah said, "Vera the pony, Pence and Jam, the sheep, and Nan and Papa the goats were the first larger animals we tanked. At that point we hadn't realised the necessity of using exoskeletons for extended periods. Vera, Pence and Jam remain the only animals we have lost as a direct result of being tanked."

"Do you know why?"

Shah said, "The only conclusion I have been able to make is that, apart from not using exoskeleton exercisers, all three were mature animals. The two goats were ten weeks old and had just been weaned."

Arblette turned her attention back to Doctor Darling and seemed to find her assertive feet again. "That is my point. Your human tanking tests have not been nearly far-ranging enough. By your own admission you have tanked subjects in excellent health and in their twenties."

Chavez said harshly, "That is because our volunteers were mostly young."

"Mostly?" She pounced.

He stared her down.

"But you have never tanked anyone my age, for example." She smiled around. "For the record, I am thirty-four."

Darling said, "We currently have two subjects over thirty in our stas-tanks. The first is —" He glanced towards Shah.

"The first is my wife, Inge. She was thirty-two when she entered the tank," Shah said.

"That's still y —"

Darling broke in, "Our second subject is chronologically forty-seven — though physically she is forty-five, having been in the tank for two years."

Arblette's face went slack with surprise.

Someone hasn't done her homework, or else has relied on intel from someone else who wasn't in possession of all the facts, Harry thought.

He felt Rachel squeeze his hand and glanced down into her questioning eyes.

He gave a tiny shrug. He wasn't in possession of all the facts, either.

Chavez said, "We expect to collect data on these two subjects within the next two years. In the meantime, we will proceed with the planned five-year extended tanking of two volunteers who have already undergone three sessions in the tanks — Doctor Harrison Fejoa and Rachel Traveller. They are here and are on schedule to enter the tanks in thirty minutes." He looked over to two blue-clad nurses who had just entered from the tank room. "That will give you time for prepping?"

They nodded and pressed through the small group towards Harry and Rachel.

"What about Field and Jonty and Sof?" Rachel whispered.

Harry looked about. He had supposed they were there somewhere, but only he and Rachel had been tagged by Chavez.

"Maybe they —" He broke off, unable to formulate a proper suggestion.

"Hello," Amber Fordyce said, drawing Harry's attention.

The second nurse introduced herself to Rachel as Ju Cho.

Well, this is an unseemly rush, Harry thought. *Maybe the other three couldn't be fetched in time.*

That made sense. No one had said they had to stay in proximity to the facility.

Rachel tightened her grasp on Harry's hand. "Amber, can we do the preps in the same room?"

"That would be—" the second nurse began, but Amber nodded.

"Yes, we'll do that, because this is a decision you two need to make together." She turned to Cho. "Harry and Rachel are an established couple. I'm sure they've seen one another naked on numerous occasions."

"We have and we've decided already. We're going to proceed," Rachel said. She added, "Before Arblette gets her claws into us."

They followed the two nurses to one of the interview cubicles. It was crowded with four people inside, but they took it in turns to sit and examine the waiver which they both signed.

Amber said, "We need a voca-sig as well. Please state your names and read this short statement . . . if you agree with it."

Rachel tapped her chip on the screen. "I am Rachel Traveller. I agree I am entering a stas-tank for the period of five calendar years. I will enter of my own free will and I understand all care will be taken by the staff of Outward Bound to maintain the tank and my health. I understand that if decisions need to be made on my behalf they will be made by my nominated champions . . . " She paused the screen. "The same as before?"

Amber nodded.

"Harry Fejoa, my fiancé, is my chosen advocate. If he is unavailable by reason of being tanked himself, I nominate Doctor Tav Shah. Should he not be able to act for me for any reason, I nominate Abra Kiev or Amber Fordyce. I am in good health and of sound mind and I understand the physical, mental and emotional implications of what I am about to do. I accept full responsibility for my decisions." Rachel touched her chip to the screen.

Harry was about to go through his voca-sig when Amber held up her hand. "Wait . . . Ju, will you take Rachel through for her shower and lotion? And Rachel, make sure you stay in the lotion a bit longer than usual. This is the big five."

The other nurse nodded.

"Where does the naked bit come in?" Harry quipped.

"You could shower together, but . . ."

Rachel smiled at Harry, moved up and gave him a long kiss. "Never mind. See you on the other side! And make sure you think of me!"

"Always," he said.

She grinned. "See you in the morning!"

Harry watched her go, then turned to Amber. "What's wrong?"

"Nothing," she said.

"What was all that palaver outside? Who is Doctor Arblette? She seemed — " He broke off and considered. " — Adversarial," he concluded.

"She's a government invigilator," Amber said in a dry tone.

"Has she any power over the project?"

"Not officially. She's supposed to be purely an observer."

"That's not the way it sounded. Have you really paused the recruiting on her say-so?"

"Yes, for a while . . . but not entirely on her say-so."

"Whose, then? Chav didn't seem too pleased."

"Chavez is *never* pleased. He's — " She caught herself up. "There is something in what she said . . . not that we have any doubts about the tanking process, but she did have a point about people losing their enthusiasm for a project that is so many years from fruition. Some of our early applicants have withdrawn."

"Rachel and I haven't lost our enthusiasm."

"Clearly. However, you are the last ones standing from a

starting sample of seventeen elites."

"Field, Sofia, and Jonty have dropped out?" That did surprise him, as well as finally solving the question of the phantom three. "I thought maybe they just hadn't got there yet."

"They're still with Outward Bound. Jonty is working with Tav. The animal tanking is proceeding because, as you may know, it was never intended as simply a failsafe before we started with humans."

"No — we're taking animals along," he agreed.

"Exactly. We want them to have the best possible experience. Tav is committed to that, and Jonty is in a useful position to see tanking from both sides. She doesn't want to miss five years of research and experience. Sofia and Field have also put their applications on ice until closer to launch. We do have my sister and the other subjects in stas though, so — " She broke off. "This is really not the time."

"I agree." Harry touched the screen, consigning his questions to the future. "I, Harrison Fejoa . . . " He went through the waiver then paused as Rachel had done. "I need to change one of my champions. Will you stand for me?"

"Yes."

"My cousin, whom you contacted for me last time, is not able to continue in her role."

She nodded, seeming unsurprised, and gestured to the screen.

Harry said, "Rachel Traveller, my fiancée is my chosen advocate. If she is unavailable, I nominate Doctor Tav Shah and should he not be able or willing to act for me, I nominate Amber Fordyce or Field Shaloman."

He touched his chip, and Amber escorted him to the tank room for the big five.

As he offered his wrist to Doctor Darling, he thought of Rachel then, fleetingly, of Inge Shah.

I should have asked how Willow —

Chapter Twenty-two: Afterimage, 2245

Harry opened his eyes and stretched, feeling for the familiar towel that had embraced him on his other de-tanking awakenings.

Instead, his arms resisted his attempt to reach down and tug at the material.

Ugh.

He tried again. This time, his arm moved, but there was more resistance than there ought to be.

He blinked in the dim light and tried to sit up.

Nothing doing.

"Hello?"

"Hello there!" The cheerful voice was familiar, but he couldn't place it in context. It wasn't Doctor Darling, or even Amber Fordyce.

"Hello," Harry said again. He added petulantly, "I'm stuck."

The voice said, "You woke a wee bit earlier than we expected. We haven't uncoupled the exoskeleton yet."

That made sense. He'd used one before, for the one-month tanking, but they must have removed it before he woke.

"Undo it now," he said.

"We need to take your vitals first and check your muscle resistance."

"My vitals are fine. Get me out of this frame."

"Keep your wig on, Harry."

Hands moved over his limbs, working catches and un-wrapping bands.

Then his attendant dropped a towel over him.

"What's up with the lights?" Harry sat up, peering about him.

"Protocol to prevent retinal damage."

"My retinas are fine. I want a shower. And breakfast. And Rachel. And not necessarily in that order."

"You can have the shower, but I do advise you to lie quietly for a bit first."

Harry braced himself and swung his legs off the bed. His head spun for a few seconds, then he got his orientation back. "I'm fine. Better than fine." He slid down to find his feet tingling a little, resisting the temptation to launch into a series of jumping jacks. "Have these beds got higher?"

"Sorry. I had you cranked up to save me bending."

"Grand. Field, right?"

"That's right," Field Shaloman said.

"What are you doing here? You're a midwife, not a de-tanker."

"I've done some extra training these last few years. I volunteered to be your midwife. So to speak."

Harry saw the analogy. "Hell of a long pregnancy — five years," he said. "Can I have enough light to see myself shower? Wouldn't do to spend five years in a tank only to impale myself on the taps or crack my head on a sprinkle-head."

Field brought up the light a few notches and Harry took himself to the shower.

As the bio-fluid and the last of the blue lotion swilled away, he looked down at himself. His skin, which might have been pallid from lack of light, looked flushed and healthy. He'd expected that. He touched his toes and tested his hand-eye coordination. All good. He washed his hair, which felt the same as usual after a tanking. When he brushed his chin he noted bristles. Of course—he was subjectively five days older than he had been when he entered the tank. His beard had had time to grow.

Better get rid of that, he thought with a grin, remembering Rachel's strictures on prickles.

Rachel. He looked up from his contemplation of the now-clear stream of water. This was her cue to join him.

He smiled, waiting. Field wouldn't care. He had *two* loving partners.

He wondered if they'd had their ceremonial linking or blessing or whatever they'd decided to do.

He waited.

No Rachel.

Shrugging, he turned off the water and got into the absorbent robe someone had given him instead of a second towel. It was all encompassing, with a hood.

Cultish, he thought, suppressing a chortle at the thought of the woollen cloaks Rachel had made from their knitted squares. He hoped someone had hung them up to air.

He left the shower room and moved back to the cubicle.

Field was tidying away used towels.

He looked older than Harry remembered. That made sense. They'd last seen one another during the field trip to *Elysian Dawn*, which was about six years ago.

Field said, "Okay, Tank Man. Now you need a nice rest and some gentle physio."

"Do I heck. You know how well we always feel after tanking."

"I remember, but it's a big jump from a month to five years. Exoskeleton notwithstanding you might have a few minor wobbles."

"Not me. Fit as a flea and twice as dangerous." He bounced on his toes to demonstrate, trod on his hem, and made a grab for a rail. "Not a *word*," he said ferociously to Field.

"Rest and gentle physio," Field said.

Harry grinned at him. "Right. Where's Rach? I expected her to seduce me in the shower. That's what happened last time we showered together." He saw Field's face change. "I expect Jonty and Sofia sometimes give you a nice morning surprise. That's if you're still together."

"We are very much together." Field spread his hands. "That's why I'm working here. Jonty and Sofe help Tav and Willow with the gang."

That made sense, he supposed. "Is Inge out of the tank?"

"Not permanently," Field said.

"What do you—"

Field continued, "She comes out for a week every year. It was decided the accumulated time wouldn't make a great deal of difference, and tank euphoria keeps her well enough to spend what she calls quality time with Tav and Willow."

"I thought the plan was to have data after two years . . . surely that's what was said to Arblette."

"There's plenty of data. Inge seems to be tolerating the tanking well."

"Yes, but—" Harry caught himself up. "Sorry, Field. The lag takes a bit of getting used to. Going in this time was a big adrenaline rush and I'm still feeling the mental effects of that."

"That's understandable." Field added, "I'll take some synapse readings and check your eyes. Are you hungry?"

About to say he was starving, Harry realised he actually wasn't. He felt incredibly well, but also a bit . . . not tired, but odd.

"Sensory overload," he suggested.

"What?" Field caught his arm and conducted him to a chair. "Sit down, Harry. I want to check your pupils."

Harry growled, "Who's the doctor here?"

"Both of us. I upskilled. Close your eyes."

Harry closed them.

"Open."

He did so and shied. "Hey!"

Field put away the tiny penlight. "Pupil response normal."

"And retinas cringing," Harry said indignantly, seeing splashes and spots before him.

"Yes — well — the afterimages will soon settle. I'll see about something for you to eat."

Harry jumped out of the chair. "Where's Rach?"

Field pressed him down again. "Will you stop hopping about? She's next door. She was tanked after you and . . . oh, give it twelve hours. Don't go barging in. In fact, lie back into the chair. I'll configure it to give you a physio-massage. Pop into one of your trances and when you wake up . . ."

Field's voice blurred and Harry lay back obediently. He knew, objectively, that the tank euphoria was more extreme this time and a spell in a light trance would help to balance his mind.

He felt the chair tilt back and begin an almost imperceptible massage of calves, shoulders, neck and . . .

Chapter Twenty-three: Seismic Shift, October 2245

Harry woke with an extraordinary sense of elapsed time. Hours, surely, if not days, had passed since he succumbed to Field's determination to settle him down.

Someone touched his cheek, gently, kindly, and familiarly, then he felt a kiss brush over his brow.

He smiled. "Rach." She was being surprisingly chaste today. Well, it *was* a long time since they'd been together. *Only yesterday.*

"No, Hazzy. It's me."

The voice was as familiar as his own.

"And me." A hand caught his.

That voice was not familiar, exactly, but it tugged at the back of his mind as someone he used to know or might have known— The hand ought to have been smaller, and sticky.

He opened his eyes to daylight. They stung and watered for a moment, but the afterimage had gone. He looked at the person standing in front of him, incongruously holding his hand—a lifeline, tethering him to the present. She was small with fair skin and straight honey-brown hair. Her eyes were . . . oh! She had segmental heterochromia of a strangely beautiful type he'd seen only once before. If he'd had any doubts, the person's tunic would have settled them immediately. It was a strong and persuasive shade of turquoise.

"Turq!" He felt a ridiculous grin spreading over his face as he contemplated his godchild.

She smiled in response, but she didn't fling herself on him

for a sticky hug.

Of course not. She was — what — Harry tried to add it up. *Born 2230, and . . .* No. That would make her fifteen, and she just wasn't. He knew the occasional girlchild remained pre-pubescent at fifteen, but Turq was a leggy sylph of eleven or so. Twelve at the most.

Ergo — he'd been woken early.

He sat forward cautiously, feeling the straps of the chair parting as it readjusted to his new position. He glanced down at himself. He was still wrapped in the towelling robe.

"What date is it?" he asked the child.

"October the seventh, twenty-two forty-five," she responded, stepping back and disengaging from his hand. "It's lunch time," she added helpfully.

So, it *was* five years later.

Fifteen, eh. Maybe her early deprivations had affected her growth. He felt a wave of regret that he had not managed cheese more often for her, and fruit and vegetables as well. Still, here she was.

The other person, the one who had kissed him, moved into view and he smiled with relief. "Flav!" He held out his arms and she came in for a hug. "It's wonderful to see you and Turq again, but how did you get here?"

"That's a long story," Flavia said.

"But not as long as it ought to be," the child put in. "What do I call you? I can't remember calling you anything, but I sort of remember you. I think. Did you use to bring me cheese?"

He nodded. "Yes, when I could. You used to call me Hazzy, but that was when you were a sticky urchin. You and I are some sort of cousins, so I should think Harry will do." He glanced at Flavia. "If that's okay with your mum."

"Harley makes her own decisions," Flavia said.

The girl nodded vigorously. "I'm emancipated."

"I'd congratulate you, but I'm wondering why . . . you

have the best mother in the world."

"I know that. She's still my mum, but I had to have my own recognisance to be allowed to sign stuff — " She broke off, then held out her hand to Harry again. "Doctor Field said we can take you to the kitchen room for something to eat." She scrunched up her nose. "Standard soup for you, he said. They always give you soup when you come out."

"Usually," Harry agreed. He accepted her hand to help him out of the chair, though he needed no help.

He was still trying to see the sticky grub he knew in this serious child.

They moved on to the next room. Harry didn't recognise it, but at least it wasn't the hospital room they had stuffed him in after the sim. It was an ordinary-looking cafeteria-style room with moulded chairs and tables and a lot of shining silver benches and appliances.

"Is this deliberately unappetising?" he asked.

Turq giggled. "Yes! All that metal is hygienic, but Doctor Field said it's also to stop people hanging around in here when they should be somewhere else. He doesn't approve of hanging about. He has a work ethic, and he inflicts it on everyone. You sit with Mum, Harry. I'll get the soup from the servery."

She let him go and walked across to an unfamiliar appliance, an emphatic daub of colour in a monochromatic room.

Harry turned to Flavia. "You look well . . . much better than when I saw you last. That was . . ."

"In thirty-three," she said. "Twelve years ago, in the strictly linear sense. The day you visited Harley and me and made your apartment over to us. That was extraordinarily generous of you, by the way."

"It didn't quite work out though," he said soberly. "I'm so sorry, Flav. I don't know if you heard, but Rach and I came to visit you — er — seven years or so ago. It was a shock to find you weren't there."

"I suppose it was."

"*He* was there. Your husband . . . well, I assume so."

She grimaced. "Not one of my better ideas. I should have had you come to visit before I said *I do*. I expect you'd have had his secret persona fileted like a haddock in the time it takes to say *sociopath*." She pursed her lips. "Incidentally, Haz . . . if you *had* met him and taken your filet knife to him, would you have told me what you found?"

"Probably. Would you have listened?"

"I honestly don't know."

He thought of his one brief meeting with Flavia's husband. Rachel had picked him for bad news in an instant.

"Still, he can't be all bad. He *is* Turq's father."

Flavia's face lit up. She leaned forward and said, "He's actually not. Shh!"

Harry felt nothing but relief.

"I'm sorry if he found you because of me," he said.

"Even if he did, you're blameless. All you did was try to help and we did have a good while living near the river." Flavia glanced at her daughter, who was coaxing a lever into action. "Luckily, Harley was down by the river counting ducks that day with a couple of older children. We'd stopped on our way home from the market. I was watching them, but Mink . . . one of the mums from up-river . . . came over and told me someone had come looking for me. It was *him*. She must have seen that wasn't good news because she said she was ever-so-sorry, but she'd told him I was at the market with Harley."

"And he said, 'who's Harley,'" Harry suggested when she paused.

Flavia turned out her hands. "Yes, apparently. Mink told him. We ran. The only thing I could think of to do was to contact the woman who'd called me about acting as your advocate. She said at the time it was a formality and very un-likely to be activated, but of course I'd agreed. After we ran, I let her know I couldn't act for you anymore because we had to disappear. She — "

"That was Amber Fordyce?" Harry suggested.

Flavia nodded. "She offered us a lifeline. If I'd make myself available for Outward Bound, I could sign a legal waiver put-ting us into their hands until or unless we agreed to dissolve the contract. They could arrange for our chips to go into hia-tus."

She stopped short as Harley approached, wheeling a trol-ley. Harry was reminded of Willow Shah, who had brought lunch for himself and Rachel back in . . . well, back on an ear-lier visit. She'd brought it on a similar trolley.

I'll make a timeline, he told himself, then realised it no longer mattered. Life would be linear now, until he and Ra-chel and their children-to-come embarked on *Elysian Dawn*. No more skipping months, let alone years . . .

More like a century or two.

Harley brought the trolley alongside. "This is yours," she said, setting a bowl of something in front of Harry. She gave him a sudden ferocious grin. "I cheated. Doctor Field said you were to have sludge soup with all the probiotics and things, but I got you the celery and mushroom soup instead. It's got carrots and ginger in it. Willow says ginger is healthy. You'll have to take responsibility for eating it, though. If you'd ra-ther play safe, I can get you the other one." She leaned for-ward and whispered, "That one is khaki, and it tastes the same as it looks. I told Doctor Field I'd *never* eat it again and he gave up and said I could go with celery and mushroom. He also said if I choked I had to do it on my own recogni-sance."

"I'm surprised you ate it even once," Harry said, pulling the soup towards him. He put a spoonful in his mouth. It was good.

"I wouldn't've, but I'd just got out of the tank—Harry, are you okay?" She pounded on his back as he spluttered and choked.

Flavia unloaded her own bowl from the trolley and sighed. "Harley, stop thumping him. He'll cough it up when he's ready. Choking on his own recognisance."

Harry perceived that was a family catch phrase. His eyes watered ferociously as the fit slowly passed.

The door opened and Field stuck his head in. "Harry—" Seeing him doubled over and clutching his ribs, he dashed over and grabbed Harry's wrist.

"I'm fine," Harry wheezed, aware his pulse was probably racing. "I inhaled when I meant to swallow."

Field said to Flavia, "You told him, then?"

She shook her head.

"Told me what?" Harry hauled in a breath and coughed again.

Celery in the windpipe? No . . . just vapor. Out of the habit of swallowing.

"It was my fault, Doctor Field," Harley said. "I got him proper soup because the khaki stuff tastes disgusting."

"And I take full responsibility for accepting it . . . I bet it's covered by the waiver, anyway." Harry unfolded himself and made a manful effort to calm his breathing. He mopped his eyes with his towelling sleeve. "I'm fine. I could have inhaled the other stuff just as easily."

Field sighed and withdrew.

Harry took another spoonful of soup and ate it with care. He finished the bowl, then looked at Harley, who had swallowed her portion and moved on to solid food. "Turq, do I understand you to mean you've been tanked?"

"Sure." She nodded. "Four years, if you add it up," she added around a piece of bread and a thick slab of cheese.

Four years.

Something fell into place with a clank. "So you really are

fifteen."

"I'm not," she said. "Not exactly. Doctor Tav says I'm a time machine and tank people need a new way of measuring age. He says I *might* say I'm eleven elapsed. Or maybe that I can just have tank birthdays as well as real ones."

Flavia said, "You know how it works, Harry. I'm also four years younger than my birth records suggest. You of all people ought to understand that. From what I hear you and that tank have a revolving door relationship."

"I do understand, but *why*? Why would you volunteer to tank yourself? I assume you did volunteer . . . Why would you tank Turq?"

"Why did you tank yourself?" Flavia countered.

"You know why. I work for Outward Bound, and I volunteered for tank testing in exchange for guaranteed benefits for me or my heir."

"Snap," Flavia said. Her gaze rested briefly on her daughter.

"But you said you wouldn't consider shipping out."

"I know and it's not an option for me, but with the increased focus on cure-coasting, it was necessary to have some older volunteers."

"And younger ones," Harley said. "So I volunteered along with Mum."

"And you let her." Harry raised an eyebrow at Flavia.

"I didn't let her. She emancipated. Tav Shah offered to look after her."

"So did Jonty and Sofe," Harley put in. "Doctor Field *swore and declared* he would never make me eat sludge soup if I lived with them and the kids."

"But she said she'd stick with me," Flavia said. "And believe me, it was the best choice we ever made."

"Our chips went dark, and we found out we can keep them that way," Harley said. "So *he* has probably given up looking for us . . . we hope." She looked straight at Harry with her beautiful eyes. "*He* is not my father, but he thinks he is."

Harry perceived this was a Gordian knot of a situation. He didn't have all the details and he thought he might be happier that way.

Flavia said, "Fortunately, I was able to transfer those funds you gave us into an investment in Outward Bound."

Harry, having gone out on a limb initially to make sure Flavia had the funds to use for herself and his goddaughter, and that they were *not* in Outward Bound's holding account, recalled suggesting she might come to work for the company. He had also provided her with a contact with Amber Fordyce. Mentally he flung up his hands. It was such a tangle.

Well, he'd have to do an Alexander and cut the knot right now. Flav and Turq were here, they were safe, and they were under their own recognisance. He'd love them forever, but necessarily at arms' length. He'd never know the end of their story, as they would not know his.

"Field said twelve hours," he said abruptly.

"For what?" Harley asked.

Harry said, "For Rachel." He had no idea what Harley knew, so he explained. "When I started working for Outward Bound, I met Rachel. She and I are going to be married."

"In twelve hours?" The child's arresting eyes widened. "Can I watch?"

"In a few weeks, and of course you can watch—well—unless something else happens to delay us. Rachel will be enchanted to meet you at last."

"I know about Rachel. She's the other five-year tanker who came out yesterday," Harley said.

"That's right. I came out of my tank first, and Field said Rach was due to come out in twelve hours. Or something." He frowned, trying to recall Field's exact words and tie them in with the child's inaccurate pronouncement.

Maybe they started the prelims yesterday and she misinterpreted it.

He turned to Flavia. "But you'd know all that, I expect. You were waiting for me."

"You've been out since last night, but we weren't allowed to see you then," Harley said brightly. "Doctor Field said you'd be asleep for twelve hours—then we could wake you with a sleeping beauty kiss. That was a joke, though."

"Oh, for—" As so often when dealing with Outward Bound, Harry felt like a chessman in someone else's game. He got up from the table abruptly. "It's been lovely to catch up with you again," he said, looking from Flavia to Harley and back. "I'll see you again soon—unless Chavez decides to ship me off to the island without warning—but right now I'm going to see Rach. We have a wedding to plan—and we'll do our darnedest to make sure you're there to throw rice at us."

"Rice?" Turq sounded doubtful.

Leaving Flavia to explain that if she chose, Harry cast his gaze round the room, discounted the door Field Shaloman had popped through and fastened his hopes on a different one.

He let himself out.

The corridor was unfamiliar, but he had a good sense of locality, so he headed for where he recalled the tanking cubicles should be.

Extraordinary! he thought as he strode along. When he and Rachel entered the tanks, Flavia and Harley must have been mere metres away. He thought back to the peculiar briefing they'd attended just before heading off to be processed.

Doctor Francesca Arblette had been posturing about age and Darling had taken her down a couple of pegs, just as Tav Shah had done regarding the animals. After the disclosure of Inge Shah's status, someone had mentioned a second mature tanker ... *that must have been Flav!* As far as he recalled, Harley hadn't been mentioned specifically ... maybe someone thought Arblette's ignorance in that matter was better all around. She'd seemed fixated on choosing *young* people, but she probably didn't want them quite as young as Harley.

Someone might have told *him* about them though.

Wait — he'd told Amber Fordyce that Flav couldn't act for him as a champion, and she'd seemed unsurprised. Obviously, she'd thought he *knew* Flav was at the facility. So — who had championed for Flav and Harley?

"Oh, hang it!" Harry muttered. No point in cutting one Gordian knot and tangling himself in another one.

He strode into the tanking area. Two techs were cleaning and prepping the tank he'd lately left. He resisted the temptation to make a quip, hoping and supposing his hooded robe hid his identity.

Who do you think you're fooling? And what could they do to you? Send you back and make you eat sludge soup?

They didn't look up, but he nodded to their peripheral vision and continued. The next several tanks were clearly in use. How many cure-coasters and testers did they have right now?

Rachel's tank . . . empty, as he'd expected, but attended by six techs all busily doing what techs did. In this case it seemed to be a dismantlement. Weird.

He peeped into the associated shower. Empty. He ducked out and passed on down the line. No doubt Rach was chafing at the bit in a darkened recovery room, being retina-tested and forced into rest and light massage when all she wanted was to surprise Harry in the shower.

He listened, half-expecting to hear her voicing her displeasure at being robbed, yes, *robbed* of a chance of a shower seduction.

Rachel loved shower seductions, and the showers at Outward Bound were enormously better than any they'd shared elsewhere.

At the end of the corridor, a nurse in blue scrubs was helping a frail-looking woman into a wheelchair. It could not be Rachel.

Harry quickened his pace. "Amber?" The nurse turned her masked face to him. It wasn't Amber, but her brown eyes widened at the sight of him. The woman in the chair stared.

"Sorry, I thought you were someone else," Harry said to both of them. "I'm looking for Rachel Traveller."

"She's in Recovery Room H," the nurse said, glancing into the next corridor. "Sir, you can't—"

"Of course I can. I'm her fiancé. And her champion." He darted past them.

"*Sir!*"

Recovery Room H was a carbon copy of the room he'd been in with Field Shaloman, but the lights were on, and several gowned figures were holding some kind of conference near the raised bed where Rachel lay.

"Rach!" Harry rushed in, scattering medics. "I've come to rescue you," he added, with thrilling drama.

He expected her to sit up and swing her legs over before rushing . . . or maybe swaying . . . into his embrace, but she didn't move.

Her skin was still streaked with blue and brown stickiness and her beautiful hair looked matted.

She must have just come out of the tank. He'd stormed in before she was properly awake.

"Rach?"

He was grabbed by the elbows and hoisted . . . dragged . . . out of the way.

It was suddenly noisy . . . and hot . . .

He hauled forward, staring. Someone was using a heart gauge. Someone was measuring blood oxygen.

Someone—

Harry wanted to scream. He was bewildered, but not. His life had been hit with a seismic shift and he understood it far too well. He was a physician, after all.

Chapter Twenty-four: Sleeping Beauty Kiss, December 2245

Someone sedated him.

Harry never found out who it was, and he didn't much care.

He couldn't even say for sure how long they kept him under.

Surfacing vaguely from time to time, he understood he was in a thera-tank, tranced down so he was *just* aware of himself.

It was Doctor Darling who got him out of it, pulling his fluid line suddenly and painfully then slapping his face to jerk him out of his stupor. "Doctor Fejoa, come with me."

"Rachel."

"Yes, I'll tell you. Come with me."

Harry almost fell as he exited the tank and Darling, losing patience, hoisted him over his shoulder, deposited him in a shower and turned on the cold water.

"Up you come." Hoisted again into a large towel then enveloped in one of the long robes, Harry was vaguely aware of being trundled in a wheelchair across open ground, up a ramp and into a room—not a hospital or a lab, but someone's sitting room.

"Couch," Darling said, and tipped him out of the chair.

Harry tottered to the couch and heard the prosaic sound of a kettle and the bite of a knife on bread.

"Let me know when you can hold a cup," Darling said.

Harry put out his hand.

"Okay. It will scald if you drop it. I can get you a feeding cup if you prefer."

"No." The first sip almost did make him drop it, but he got down half a cupful. It was tea, much weaker than he liked.

"Let me know when you're ready to listen."

Harry set the cup down on the occasional table beside him with exaggerated caution. Then he looked up.

Darling looked back with his cold, expressionless eyes. Whatever he saw in Harry's must have satisfied him because he nodded and sat back in an armchair, facing the couch. "I'm going to tell you what happened. You are going to listen sensibly. If you go into a meltdown, I'll sedate you and have someone put you back in the thera-tank. I will regret this intervention and I won't make another one. Do you understand?"

"Yes."

"Right. It wasn't my idea to put you down initially. The theory was that elapsed time would give you some perspective. In my private opinion, the elapsed time was to buy breathing space for others, not for you. I want you to understand I'm acting on my own behalf here in taking you out of the thera-tank. Your appointed advocates have been dithering about wanting what's best for you. I don't want what's best for you, particularly. I want what I think is right. What I would want in your shoes. Do you understand?"

Harry nodded and reached shakily for the cup.

"Good. Drink that and tell me if you want more."

Harry sipped the cooling liquid in tiny increments. He didn't feel up to another choking fit.

Darling nodded with seeming approval. "As you know, we tanked you and Ms Traveller as scheduled five years ago. Everything was done rather quickly on account of an influx of . . . unrest . . . but it was done in accordance with correct procedure. I will swear to that. Everything was monitored as usual. You were, and are, the longest-term tanked subjects. Others have been tanked for nearly as much or even more *real* time, but they have been brought out at intervals. Tav Shah's toad, for example. Theoretically, he may be still alive in a century or more, but eventually he will die of old age. In a hundred years he will age around three months, but once we add the two weeks of ex-tank time he enjoys every year, the aging will accumulate."

Harry made an abrupt gesture, almost spilling his remaining tea.

He wasn't here to listen to Darling ramble on about Toodles the toad. He thought back to the initial lecture the viabilities had suffered from Darling, who had wanted to focus on thera-tanking while they wanted to know about the long-term tanks.

It had taken a few pointed interruptions to get him onto the correct track.

Darling might have remembered it too. He thinned his already thin lips and continued. "I gather you felt well and normal when you emerged from the tank."

"I did." *A hell of a lot better than I feel now.* He was weak and shaken and tank euphoria was a distant memory. He felt . . . old.

"I brought you out and handed you over to my colleague when your respiration and heart rate returned to sleep normal. I was surprised at how quickly that happened. I understand you surfaced before the exoskeleton could be released. Doctor Shaloman reported that you continued to respond in a manner he assured me was normal — for you. With grumpiness and a desire to leapfrog his recommendations and dash off somewhere, that is.

"Having given you into his care, I de-tanked Ms Traveller. Once again, everything went to the usual routine. Her heart rate and breathing began to rise on schedule but — " He broke off, leaned in and removed Harry's cup from his grip before setting it down gently. "Her recovery stalled. Harry, she hasn't woken."

"Field made me sleep in his damned massage chair."

"I'm aware of that. We needed to keep you relaxed until we had clear facts to tell you. However, Ms Traveller—"

"Rachel. Rach."

"Rachel did not wake. She showed no signs of returning consciousness."

The silence stretched.

"She is breathing, albeit slowly and with augmented oxygen. Her heart is beating, but she has no brain activity beyond the baseline needed for unconscious systems."

Harry clenched both fists.

"Harry, I am sorry. That is not an apology. I have gone over and over the procedure. The tank has been examined minutely. Everything is textbook—except that Rachel has not shown any vestige of awareness."

Harry felt cold. He heard his own voice coming from a long way off. "She sometimes takes quite a while to come out of trance. It worried me the first time, but now I know to just wait. She opens her eyes when she's ready—comes from unresponsive to wide awake in the snap of your fingers. When she's had enough of her beautiful nothingness she comes back to me."

After more silence, he added, "It's been just a few hours."

Well, twelve.

"No, Harry. It's been two months."

Harry's mind insisted thera-tanking was unsafe for more than a few days.

No wonder he felt so ill.

Someone had been irresponsible and should be dismissed.

He couldn't be bothered to say so.

He looked mutely into Darling's chill gaze. "Rach likes you."

The man blinked.

"She says you're a decent person—and maybe shy. She says you make sure she's modestly in the tank before you approach to fix her cannula."

Darling lifted a shoulder. "I'm sorry to give you this unwelcome news."

"Well." Harry struggled to his feet. "Thank you for telling me. And for getting me out of the damned thera-tank."

"It seemed the right thing to do."

"It was. Mind, that's the only thanks you're getting from me. And it's a deal more than anyone else is due. Who decided to thera-tank me anyway?"

Darling said nothing. Either he didn't know, or professional solidarity was keeping him silent.

"*Was* it you?"

"I told you it was not."

Harry stared at him for a few seconds. "Then I believe you. Never mind. It's not as if I can do anything about it. I would like to know what my *champions* were doing, though. Well, I know what *Field* was doing. Keeping me out of the way until someone could ambush me. Did Flavia know?"

"No. Only that there was a delay."

"I should have chosen you as my champion." Harry walked to the door, then swung round. "Nothing to say?"

"I've said it," Darling said. "You're welcome to stay here until you feel ready to do whatever comes next." He got up from his chair. "I have to go back to work. You are free to go and do what you choose—as long as you don't endanger anyone under my care." He opened the door and stepped through past Harry. "If you feel like food, there's bread and cheese . . . real cheese. Tav's goats have been uncommonly fecund."

Harry shot out a hand and grabbed his shoulder. "Not so fast."

Darling stepped back in, and Harry forced himself to let go. "Please . . . I need to see her. I'm her champion."

"I'll take you to her, but remember what I said."

"No meltdowns."

"No rages or accusations either. Harry, you *must* appear equable."

Harry scowled.

"For your own sake, and for Rachel's. If you show signs of being unbalanced, you could be removed from Rachel's championship and lose your own recognisance."

"To appear balanced in this circumstance is sure proof of being unbalanced," Harry said.

"That's probably true. I suggest you choose the demeanour that you consider natural . . . then err on the side of calm."

Harry gave a jerky nod. "I need proper clothing."

"I brought it here before I got you out of the thera-tank. It's in the next room. Go and make yourself presentable."

Harry went through to a laundry room where he found the clothing he had worn to the facility five years before. It was all there, aside from his patchwork cloak. He dressed and combed his hair, then used a razor he found in a package. Rachel didn't care for bristles.

He joined Darling, who had apparently filled in the time with more tea and a sandwich he was just finishing. "There's one for you if you want." He inclined his head to the bench a few paces away.

Harry rejected that. "I'd throw up."

"You have nausea?"

"Yes. It's psychological. I'd be unbalanced if I didn't feel sick."

"We can wait if you'd prefer. I don't feel comfortable taking you anywhere with nothing but weak tea in your system."

"It was exceedingly weak," Harry agreed.

"Denatured. No one can get the good stuff anymore. Shall

we sit down until you feel able to eat?"

Harry stepped across and bit into the bread and cheese. He chewed and swallowed. His stomach lurched, then settled. He took another bite. "Satisfied?"

"Yes. You are showing reasonable reactions and good sense. Bring it with you."

Harry followed Darling outside.

"This is the wrong way," he said.

"We've moved Rachel to a high-dependency ward," Darling said. "It wasn't possible to continue caring for her in the recovery room." They entered another door in the facility and walked to a bank of lifts. "Top floor," Darling said. He tapped in a code and the lift ascended. "You're an attached medical specialist, if anyone asks," he told Harry.

The lift slowed and they walked onto a floor Harry hadn't visited before. It was quiet, aside from the faint hum and beep of medical equipment. Two people in scrubs walked past.

Harry, still chewing the last bite of sandwich, walked after Darling. He expected another mini lecture, but Darling just waved his hand at a sensor and let them into a ward.

There were three patients in the high white and chrome beds, but Harry was interested only in Rachel.

Someone had washed her. No vestige of the brown bio-fluid or blue skin conditioner was visible. Her hair was covered with a blue cap. Harry hoped they hadn't shaved her head. She wanted to be Rapunzel for their wedding.

Sensors on her chest, temples and fingers were of the minimalist type, and the oxygenator was translucent and barely visible. The faint sigh hovered just on the edge of audibility. The blip of her heartbeat was sluggish but regular.

Harry approached, reining in his desire to dash to her side and fling himself down to weep. One dose of knock-out juice was enough.

A nurse standing by the bed moved away at a signal from

Darling.

Harry stepped up, forcing himself to look over the read-ings, as if she was some other patient.

But this was Rachel.

He turned to Darling. "Have you tried bringing her breath-ing into line with normal patterns?"

"Yes. It distressed her body into arrhythmia. It's taken a while to get this balance. She's stable and somehow it's enough."

Harry took her hand, hoping for the slightest pressure to show she was aware of his presence. "Rach." He leaned over her.

It was a cliché, but other than the sensors, she looked to be asleep.

You'd better kiss her, Harry.

It was Genevieve Brant's voice, echoing back from their time in the sim.

That's the traditional way to wake a sleeping beauty.

He bent and kissed her with all his love and longing.

CHAPTER TWENTY-FIVE: SIDES-TO-MID-DLE, DECEMBER 2245 – JANUARY 2246

Rachel never stirred.

Harry knew, in that moment of kissing her, that she was gone, "outward bound," so far away she might never find her way back.

He gathered himself together, pulling in and tucking down.

Later, he thought it was like kneading dough, something he'd done on both islands, turning it sides-to-middle, over and over. He took Harry the lover, the part of him that was Rachel's alone, and turned it in, folding it like butter until it was cloistered in the loaf of himself.

When he straightened he looked at Rachel as the patient, the subject, the medical puzzle.

"Have you some scans so I can do comparisons?" he asked.

Darling breathed out softly but audibly. "They're all available in the hub." He indicated a palm-sized device. He added, "It was developed a couple of years ago—a multi-diagnostic and storage facility. It has holographic capability. Just hover your finger over the H-button, then use your fingers to expand or contract."

Harry cautiously did so, approving the concertina file system cross-referenced with date, time and variation.

"She's stable," he agreed, examining the breathing and heartbeat data.

He turned to the third comparison and didn't like it.

"We're taking another full scan in early January," Darling said. "If her brain activity fades much more —" He broke off.

"Then you'll do another scan the next month," Harry supplied.

"There may not be any point. If the next one follows the current trend, another month may see it undetectable."

"Yet she's able to breathe alone."

"Yes. The support is simply there to give her brain the best chance."

Harry handed over the hub and took Rachel's hand. "Rachel."

He didn't ask if she could hear him. He could have accessed the hub and watched the brain activity in real time, to see if it reacted to his voice, but he didn't.

He squeezed her fingers gently. The skin was soft and her flesh firm and yielding. She was in perfect condition.

Rach, are you in there?

Because he was desperate, he did something he'd always resisted.

Holding her hand, he closed his eyes. "You're moving gently out of the daylight into a vast wide emptiness, pricked with stars. Clouds of mist float gently like wedding veils as you're drifting outward bound."

He continued to murmur, holding her hand but now concentrating on putting himself into a standing trance, then walking out to join her.

He moved into the starry emptiness he had never visited before, not in a hurry, letting it take him gently away.

He'd never much liked the idea of the place he and Rachel had made for her mind, but now he almost saw why Rachel loved it. The vast dome of the sky was airy and somehow light, gentle as a kiss and majestic as a thundercloud. He drifted on, walking on nothing, but aware of the lap and sigh of an ocean somewhere beyond. He was tempted to populate the strip of land with palms and sun-warmed rocks giving back the heat of the day.

He resisted the urge. This wasn't Honeymoon Island. It was Rachel's glorious emptiness.

Rach, are you here?

Why would you ask that?

If you are, come home.

Not yet. I'm outward bound.

The imagined conversation left him crying, as he shifted back to the waking plane.

Darling had his back turned. Embarrassment or consideration?

Harry mopped his eyes on his upper arm and gently released Rachel's hand.

He wouldn't visit her emptiness again. If she *was* in there, she was somewhere he couldn't reach.

She moved.

He gasped.

Darling turned and put his hand on Harry's. "It's the ripple effect . . . the bed."

"Of course." His voice sounded choked. He put his shoulders back. "I want to be present at the next scan."

"You will be."

Darling gave no other words of comfort or reassurance.

Harry went back to work. With his new knowledge, he was able to assist with the patients who arrived for cure-coasting. He spent some time with True Tale, the woman he had seen in the wheelchair. She was a candidate for the tank and Harry was in charge of monitoring her state of mind. She never mentioned that day they'd met, and he had no idea if she recognised him anyway.

He thought how much Rachel would have liked her name.

He spent his downtime at Darling's cottage or with Flav and Harley, and once with Willow Shah. Willow was seventeen now, working full time with the animals of Outward

Bound.

To Harry, she had matured with a leap. The difference a few years made was far more noticeable in Willow than with anyone else he knew, aside from Harley.

Willow had grown into a reticent young woman, friendly and polite. She could no longer be made happy simply by praising her cooking.

She told Harry her mother had seemed well during her last de-tanking, which had occurred six months before.

"She seems to find it uncomfortable talking to me. She loves me and all, but she can't keep up. She asks me about things she remembers from last time . . . which is yesterday to her . . ." Her voice trailed off and she shrugged. "At least we can talk about Kanga. She helped to choose him, and I can still ride him."

Willow looked down at her hands, which were engaged with measuring bran mash into buckets.

"When Mum first went into the tank, we thought it would be for just a few years. *Out before you know it.* When we realised it was going to be longer, they said she could come out every year for a week or so. That should make it better for Dad and me . . . as if she's come for a holiday with us. The trouble is, we have news, but she doesn't, so we do all the talking. When she does mention something, it's yesterday for her, but sometimes we've forgotten. Still — it's better than nothing."

She clattered the lid onto the wooden barrel where the bran was stored.

"Dad says she'd be gone by now if it wasn't for tanking. It's hard on him." Willow apparently recalled Harry's own situation, because she said, quietly, "It's hard on you too, Harry. I remember how kind you and Rachel were when you came to see us before Mum was tanked the first time."

"We meant to come back to visit, but by the time we had a

chance, your mum had gone into the tank."

"Yes. She was going to wait a year, but she started getting worse. The idea is for her to be as strong as possible when the cure comes." She shrugged. "It was better while Amber was here."

"She's not now?" Harry was startled. He hadn't sought out Amber Fordyce because he was angry over his champions' lack of support for him.

Dithering, as Doctor Darling had put it.

Willow shook her head. "No. She left. She still comes to see us, but she said she couldn't deal with the board anymore. Not after—" She broke off. "I think really, she couldn't deal with *us* anymore. Dad's so upbeat, which she can't understand. I'm starting to look more like Mum and that bothers her. She looks at me and tears up." She grimaced. "Second thoughts, maybe it *wasn't* better when she was here. At least Dad and I get to have a laugh without feeling bad about it. Never mind. I have to go and feed the ponies. I'd invite you to come, but I'm sure you're busy."

Harry agreed that he was.

The days slipped by. Rachel's condition seemed stable. Harry resisted the urge to read the information in the hub every morning.

He kissed Rachel on every visit. No one tried to stop him. He was grateful, but he was afraid it meant they had written her off.

She would go on breathing with the respiration aid, and her heart would go on beating, but if her brain activity dropped much more she would be unrecoverable.

That wouldn't have happened by the upcoming scan.

It would *never* happen. Harry would not allow it.

The day of the scan came. Harry expected a cluster of medics and assistants, but what he got was Darling.

"Are you ready?"

The man's eyes were never more than cold.

Harry took Rachel's hand. "Okay, Rach. We're going to check you over."

Darling switched off the respirator.

Harry held his breath and Rachel's hand. Her pulse continued its steady sluggish beat. Her breaths continued slow and low and even.

Darling measured oxygenation of her blood.

"Well?"

"A tiny change. That is extraordinary."

"Rach *is* extraordinary." Harry paused a beat. "But it is failing?"

"No. If anything, there a slight improvement."

Gently, he opened one of her eyes. "No pupil dilation. Are you ready for the brain activity scan?"

Harry wasn't, but he nodded. Darling handed him the hub. "Usually, we simply observe the screen printout. This time, we're running a deep scan. When you're ready."

Harry attached sensors to Rachel's temples and turned on the scan.

They ran it for half an hour, during which time the bed cycled from warm to cold, and the room from light to dark. The bedframe tilted and straightened. A strong smell of ammonia came and went, followed by the aroma of baking bread and frangipani, burning rubber and old sweat. A thunderclap sounded, then came stirring music. Crickets chirped. A kettle squealed.

The scan done, Darling gestured for Harry to examine the results, alongside a comparison.

Again, he offered no comfort or encouragement. The scan told Harry what he had dreaded and what Darling had evidently expected.

"She's fading." His voice felt robotic.

"She is." Darling took Rachel's right hand and examined it.

He added, "I have no advice for you, Harry. Usually, we would discuss turning off life support at this juncture, but Rachel is breathing on her own. We might also withhold nourishment but—" He shrugged. "If she were my mate, I think I'd leave off the support but continue the feeding and let her go when she's ready. You know she's not in pain."

Harry concentrated on breathing. He felt he was suffocating.

Darling continued, "The problem is, we need to debrief representatives of the board. I don't think they will interfere with your wishes . . . but I'll leave you now to decide what those wishes are."

Harry said, "I'd like to do a circulation scan. The oxygenation is *improved*. It's a positive change."

"That is just a blip on the radar, but—as you wish. A full body scan can do no harm and it will give us a snapshot of Rachel's organs. If she is going into catastrophic organ failure—"

"She's not," Harry said sharply. "Look at her! She's perfect."

"She is. And you're right. Her skin tone is exceptional. It might be a residual effect of the bio-fluid."

Harry dragged in a breath. "Doctor Darling, if the scan shows no organ failure, I want to put Rach back in the tank. That will preserve her brain activity at the level it's at now."

"Or shut it down for good," Darling said.

"That's a risk she'd take."

"Unfortunately, it's not a risk Outward Bound will take."

"What?"

Darling spread his hands. "Harry, we have never lost a human in the tank. Tav Shah has never lost an animal, since those first ones. The company *cannot* risk a death in vitro. Rachel's condition is an anomaly. She has lived, with minimal breathing support, for three months post-tanking. However, her condition is terminal, and to put her back in the tank, slowing her back to stasis, will almost certainly kill her."

"All the cure-coasters are terminal," Harry snapped. "True has about six months, if she decides against tanking."

"Indeed, but we encourage them to enter the stas-tank as soon after diagnosis as possible. Ms Tale is not doing herself any favours by havering. You *must* see the difference."

"I want Rach tanked. I'm her champion . . . her advocate."

Darling said, "Harry, I warned you what will happen if you have a meltdown. You will be put in a thera-tank for your own protection."

Harry bared his teeth.

Cornered, he turned his back on Darling and prepared a full body scan of his beloved. He prayed for a miracle.

Chapter Twenty-six: Sea Change, January- 2246

Harry went to face representatives of the board with a depth of resolve he had never felt before.

He planned to set aside all regrets and all his pain and to make his proposition coolly and calmly.

As he expected, Landon Chavez chaired the board, but it had apparently undergone a sea change since the last time Harry had encountered it.

Chavez had been the youngest of what Harry thought of as *the major players*. Now he was markedly the eldest of the four board members present.

Harry took a few seconds to feel insulted at the low turn-out.

"What's going on? I expected to see you, Chavez, but where are Woo and Ash and Conti and the others?"

"We're here, and two others are coming." The dark-haired young woman in the blue cheongsam leaned forward. "We've met before, Doctor Fejoa."

He eyed her doubtfully. "Samantha Woo?"

"Yes. I was elected to the board when my father retired four years ago." She waved a hand to the other two strangers. "These are my colleagues Cornelia Conti and Tomas Ash, also legacy members. We've all grown up with Outward Bound."

Retired? Harry wondered how that had come about. Back in the first interview with Chavez he'd been told the current board intended to see *Elysian Dawn* from keel to launch.

The pair nodded to him. Conti was a slimmer, drabber, younger version of her aunt. Ash... Harry had no idea where he fitted in. He looked nothing like Bindilina Ash, whose surname he shared, being thin, dark-haired, pale, and intense whereas she was redhaired, cheerful, and talkative. He wondered where the relationship came in.

"You said others were coming?" Harry asked after a brief and unproductive silence.

On cue, the door slid open silently, and two more people filed in. The man was tall, distinguished-looking, greying, and unfamiliar. The other — Harry almost groaned.

"What's she doing here?" he asked Chavez. He didn't try to keep the hostility out of his voice.

Francesca Arblette smiled at him, displaying smug dimples he recalled too well. "I am attached to the board as a logistics adviser, Doctor Fejoa."

I'll just bet you are, Harry thought.

Tomas Ash said, "We're all committed to First Launch, Doctor Fejoa, as much as our mentors were, if not more. As Samantha said, we've grown up with *Elysian Dawn*."

Harry swung his attention away from Arblette. "Well, so am I committed, if you're talking about shipping out. But today I'm here on another matter."

"You're here because we summoned you," Chavez corrected.

In the twelve years Harry had known him, the man had barely changed. He had probably looked older than his calendar age during their initial interview. Today he probably looked younger. The last time they'd met, Chavez was being harassed by Francesca Arblette. Harry had hoped he'd got rid of her.

"You are here to be debriefed," Chavez added.

"That can wait. I've had more debriefings than you've had hot dinners. I'm here because Rachel needs to go back in the tank."

"Not possible," Chavez said.

"It's perfectly possible. You have already had her tanked four times—and me also. That was for your company's convenience. She now needs to go back in for our convenience. I shall go in as well, though not immediately, and stay in until someone works out a way to reverse what happened to her on *your* company's watch, which will have to be sometime within the next seven years."

Chavez shook his head. "We are aware of your unfortunate circumstances, Doctor Fejoa, but we cannot comply with your request."

"You can and you will. I am Rachel's champion. You accepted that appointment. I agreed to act for her in the event that she is unable to act—"

"Stop!" Chavez said.

"No, I'm having my say. Rachel needs to go back in the tank. I'll go back in for up to seven years. I'll then come out and debrief a final time before we board *Elysian Dawn*. If Rachel is back to normal, we'll go together. If not—"

Chavez said heavily, "Doctor Fejoa! Listen to me. There is now no question of you or Ms Traveller shipping out in First Launch."

Harry blinked. "You can't do that! We have contracts, and we have both complied with everything you've asked of us."

"We acknowledge that, but the situation has changed."

"That's not our doing."

The younger man, Tomas Ash, said, "Doctor Fejoa, you've been out of the loop for a long time—more than five years. When you entered the tank for your five-year stint you signed a waiver. Outward Bound in turn agreed to take all due care of you and Ms Traveller while you were in stasis. This was done."

Harry nodded, acknowledging this. He was sure Doctor

Darling had been truthful when he said Rachel had been treated exactly as he had been.

"However, while you were in stasis, our policies changed. You were made aware of this likelihood before you entered the tank."

"I was not!" Harry snapped.

Chavez touched a panel and a screen bloomed into being.

Harry saw himself with Amber Fordyce. She was clad in blue scrubs. For a moment, the scene hovered, then came to life.

Harry's voice said, *"That's not the way it sounded. Have you really paused the recruiting on her say-so?"*

Amber's response came clearly. *"Yes, for a while . . . but not entirely on her say-so."*

Harry's voice said. *"Whose, then? Chav didn't seem too pleased."*

"Chavez is never pleased. He's – " Amber broke off, before continuing. *"There is something in what she said . . . not that we have any doubts about the tanking process, but she did have a point about people losing their enthusiasm for a project that is so many years from fruition. Some of our early applicants have withdrawn."*

Harry watched the scene play through until the last few words.

"We do have my sister and the other subjects in stas though, so – " Amber seemed to lose her train of thought. *"This is really not the time."*

"I agree." Harry watched himself touch the screen within the screen. *"I, Harrison Fejoa . . ."*

The scene cut off and the virtual screen collapsed in on itself.

"So?" Harry said. He supposed Chavez and Arblette might have found his and Amber's comments offensive but if so, it served them right for spying.

"The point is you *were* made aware of the change in policy. You heard Doctor Arblette's comments, and you discussed it afterwards with one of your champions. You *knew* we had already ceased interviewing candidates."

"I knew there was a hiatus," Harry corrected.

"You also knew there was a shift towards a younger intake."

"You pointed out yourself that your first successful applicants were all young," Harry said.

"At the time, yes." Chavez scowled and said harshly, "There's no point prolonging this unfortunate exchange. Doctor Fejoa, Outward Bound thanks you for your contribution to the *Elysian Dawn* project, but you will not now be travelling to Magellan Sixteen."

"I have a contract that says I will! So has Rachel."

"That contract was drawn up in good faith according to the situation as we understood it at the time. Your experience notwithstanding, we're now convinced long-term tanking of humans for anything *other* than cure-coasting is too risky. One has only to look at what happened to Rachel Traveller. She was in good health and there were no contra-indications when she entered the tank. She had experienced shorter periods of time in stasis-tanks with no ill effects. Yet the extended five-year term has proved fatal."

"She's not dead," Harry growled.

Chavez disregarded that. "You have survived, but a fifty percent chance of death through irreversible brain damage is far too high a risk to be tenable. And that's after a mere five years. Consider the century-plus the colonists would be tanked. There would have been a high risk that none of them would have woken. We could not send a thousand healthy people to their probable deaths. That fact — that strong indication that *no one* could survive even ten years in a tank — is enough to negate any decisions we made while we believed it was a viable option."

"So what — you're not scrapping the project. You said you

were still committed to First Launch. What *is* First Launch, anyway? We always called it *shipping out.*"

Chavez said, "*Elysian Dawn* will be the first interstellar colony ship to launch. We are locked into that. However, we've been informed that two other ships are in the pipeline — being fast-tracked — riding on the shoulders of *our* research and development." He actually pounded his fist on his desk. "We cannot prevent them from building starships, but we will *not* let them steal First Launch."

"But you've just explained why it's not happening," Harry said blankly. He resisted glancing at Arblette, on whose shoulders he unhesitatingly placed the blame for this shift in policy.

Chavez continued, without acknowledging his comment, "Thus we have decided *Elysian Dawn* will serve as a generational colony ship."

Arblette said smoothly, "Those who board her for First Launch will do so in the transparent knowledge that they will never land on any planet. Instead, they will live and work as a closed community, carrying out duties to make themselves wholly self-sufficient. Skills will be passed down the generations to ensure the descendants that *do* land will understand what to do when they reach their new home."

Harry felt a flash of hot disappointment before rallying once more.

"Fine. So we won't travel in tanks. Rachel and I will still ship out."

"There is no question of that." Arblette folded her hands and leaned forwards.

"Rubbish," Harry said.

"It has been decided, in consultation with several experts, that the entire force of the colonists-elect will be young adults, and young dependent children."

"Rach and I are young adults . . . Chavez can tell you our

biological ages are at least five years less than the calendar suggests, and when we return to the tanks we'll remain our current biological ages—"

"Which are?" Arblette enquired.

As if you didn't know.

Harry paused to work it out. "I'm thirty-two-or-three. Rach is twenty-eight."

"That rules you out by quite a big margin. No adult older than twenty-five on launch date will be travelling and no child older than five. This has been decided to allow the colonists to ship out free of the baggage of history. They will have been carefully chosen to have no prejudices, no enmities and no so-called life experience to weigh them down."

She sat back, smiling slightly.

Harry ignored her. Focusing on Chavez, he said, "How very interesting. You've let your precious company be infiltrated. If I cared, I might suggest you should watch your back. But never mind that. Forget about First Launch. Rachel needs to be put back in the tank."

"No," Chavez said. "We are not now proceeding with tanking our colonists, but this facility is still taking in cure-coasting subjects. We cannot allow our clean record to be harmed. I'm informed Ms Traveller cannot recover, but that, having survived three months, her death will not be *directly* attributed to being in the tank. The cause of death will be *persistent vegetative state.* I must also remind you that she signed a waiver, completely of her own volition."

Unforgivably, in Harry's view, Chavez reactivated his screen.

Rachel, his lovely Rachel, in the bloom of happiness and health, appeared in freeze frame. "*I am Rachel Traveller . . .*"

Harry heard a gasp. He thought it came from Samantha Woo and Cornelia Conti, but he kept his gaze fixed on Rachel.

" . . . I am in good health and of sound mind and I understand the physical, mental and emotional implications of what I am about to do. I accept full responsibility for my decisions."

His love vanished, but Chavez reiterated, "*I accept full responsibility for my decisions.* We upheld our end of the bargain, taking all possible care of her. That waiver removes any responsibility —"

The younger women gasped again.

Harry said, "I was told you might say that. However, I have information you lack that negates this attempt of yours to duck your duty." He glanced quickly at Arblette, whose lack of proper information had discomforted her on their only previous encounter.

Had the situation not been so desperate, Harry thought he would have enjoyed serving up his news. As it was, he shot it like an arrow, right through the woman's consequence.

"Rachel did sign the waiver. I'm not disputing that. However, our child did not. And you have *no* right to endanger him at all, let alone condemn him to death."

CHAPTER TWENTY-SEVEN: FALLOUT, FEBRUARY 2246

The fallout from Harry's announcement was explosive. Arguments and counterarguments batted back and forth. Harry, armed with rage, determination, and information from Doctor Darling, countered every objection that Chavez and Arblette raised over a two-week period. He was in the fight of his life, for Rachel's chance and for their hope of a family.

The question of viability was raised. Their child was at the three-month stage and so, Arblette declared, couldn't be considered a viable entity.

Harry pointed out that conception had taken place more than five years previously.

She scoffed at that. IVF children fertilised from the same batch were often born years apart. No one tried to pretend the younger child was the same age as the elder.

Ah, but *this* child was not an IVF child. He had been conceived naturally . . . and more than five years previously. He was chronologically of an age to begin formal education.

Then Ms Traveller could be kept on life support and the child born at term.

No, Harry said. That would kill Rachel. His child was going to be born of a viable mother or not at all . . . He would not sacrifice one for the other.

He was aware that his arguments were often contradictory. He tossed the dice yet again in the knowledge that publicity of Rachel's condition and the threat to their baby would damage Outward Bound's reputation.

"You signed an NDA," Chavez said coldly.

"If our guaranteed position on *Elysian Dawn* can be set aside simply because you *changed your mind,* so can the NDA," Harry retorted.

"This change of mind has strong science behind it. We now have evidence human colonists would not survive the pro-longed time in the tanks."

"Then you can let us travel with the ones you do send. This upper age of twenty-five has *no* scientific justification. It's an arbitrary cut-off. As I recall, Bao Woo suggested — rightly — that maturity and wisdom would be valuable assets in a new community."

"Our policy is set."

"So is our contract. Either you give us what was guaran-teed in our contract or else the contract is void — and the NDA with it. You can't have it both ways."

For a while Harry thought the deadlock would remain. He had given up on shipping out. He would never go without Rachel.

His obsession now was a commitment to getting Rachel back in the tank. He would use any leverage he could think of.

He had tossed the dice in the hope it would arrest Rachel's brain's decline and allow her baby to develop slowly but safely until she might be roused, and the baby born at term. The pregnancy might be the longest one on record, but until Rachel could be woken, the place for their joint creation was with his mother.

Chavez was equally committed to *not* letting Rachel back in the tank. He would *not* risk her death in vitro.

Finally, the grey-haired man from the board came to Harry with a compromise.

"This offer is *off the record,*" he said, eyeing Harry with cold pale eyes and unveiled exasperation.

Harry prepared to be very, very difficult.

But—the offer was surprisingly good.

In exchange for a second NDA which was to remain in force until after First Launch, Outward Bound would pay the entirety of the agreed sum for both Harry and Rachel. They would sell Harry the tanks he and Rachel had used for scrap price under the fiction of upgrading their equipment.

The tanks, the grey man assured him, had been examined minutely. They were sound.

"What else?" Harry asked suspiciously. He tried, and failed, to remember the man's name, concluding he had probably never learned it.

"Obviously, this offer is on condition that you will not return to this facility, or to any other campus of Outward Bound. You will not say, write, or do anything to adversely affect the company, its personnel, *Elysian Dawn* or to jeopardise First Launch."

"Obviously," Harry said dryly. "Unless, of course, I change my mind."

"Doctor Fejoa, I hope very much that you won't do that."

"*You* did."

"I did not. I have been a major shareholder in the company for many years, but I have always left policy making to others."

"Why? You seem quite good at it, if this offer is your construction."

The man said, "I am, and it is. I have other interests, and I dislike the limelight."

"Then why come to me with this offer?"

"I thought it was the right thing to do. The alternative is to let this fight go on and on doing a lot of damage to everyone concerned."

"Especially to Rachel and our baby."

"I agree. I have never met your Rachel, but I have seen her voca-sig and spoken to those who have worked with her. I hope — and indeed, I pray — that your determination is justified and successful." He held out his hand.

"Thank you." Harry accepted it. Then he signed.

The grey-haired man counter-signed and Harry discovered his name was Diggory Dashiel Darling.

It was probably not a coincidence.

February 2247

The Rachel Foundation

A year after kissing Rachel one last time and restoring her to the tank, Harry Fejoa lay in a bath of blue lotion.

A lot could happen in a year when one was determined, ruthless and in possession of a great deal of credit.

Harry had worked harder than ever before in his life, taking accelerated learning, making plans and setting things in motion.

The Rachel Foundation occupied the old hotel complex on Brierly Island, which Harry had purchased from the less than engaged owners, using a broker. One wing now housed six tanks — four new and two refurbished. The foundation grew much of its own food in the fertile soil of the island, and those who lived and worked there had the option of tuning out their chips.

Medical researchers spent time in rotation, and a full-time practical, financial and legal staff kept the foundation's wheels turning.

Harry had spent six months hiring the best staff he could. Some he already knew and trusted — others were strangers. He interviewed every one of them himself.

Flavia was in overall charge of his personal affairs. She had withdrawn her funds from Outward Bound and, despite

Harry's demur, had reinvested in The Rachel Foundation.

Lolly Paringo had arrived the day after Harry called her, travelling light with a small bag and a huge smile.

"What do you need me to do?" she asked, reaching up on her toes to hug him.

"You're my official spirit lifter," he told her, having just decided on that.

"Your what?" She stood back and laughed, showing tiny lines in the corners of her eyes. She must be . . . what? Thirty-something, Harry concluded. Around his age, probably, but she was scarcely taller than Harley.

"Spirit lifter," he repeated. "Floating pedlar of joy and nonsense. Official cuddler of cows."

"Sounds annoying," she said.

"It's serious. The Rachel Foundation is all about hope for the future. I'm not asking you to *cheer people up.* Just be there, being you."

"That I can do. There's no one better at being Lolly Paringo than Lolly Paringo is."

"Exactly."

Tav Shah still worked for Outward Bound, but he sent Willow to help set up Harry's growing selection of livestock, augmenting the few goats and poultry left over from the viability team's tenure. They'd been allowed to go feral, but Willow soon had them feeling domesticated again. Harley became Willow's apprentice.

Doctor Darling resigned from Outward Bound the day Harry signed his agreement. He reported that no one was pleased with him for missing Rachel's pregnancy before she entered the tank—and *no one* included his uncle.

"We didn't know about it either," Harry excused himself.

"You must have known it was a possibility," Darling said dryly.

"Rach had an implant—" And there, when they finally

worked it out, lay the solution to the puzzle. Rachel's seven-year implant had quietly timed out while her chip, inactivated sporadically, thought it had some months left to go.

Harry wondered which shower seduction had resulted in their child.

He wanted to discuss the matter with Rachel.

It had been a busy year.

And now, with the foundation gathering momentum, reports on medical breakthroughs flowing in from scattered colleagues and a growing network of spies, with Flavia and Harley safe and well-occupied, his staff positive and working hard, and with so much unfinished business . . . Harry was bowing out.

"De-tank me if anything useful happens," he told Darling as he lay in the lotion bath. "If anyone needs cure-coasting, or if anyone applies to join the foundation, assess each case on its merits. Leave me a backup of everything that happens, and make sure someone responsible knows about it in case you drop dead before I do."

Darling was eating a sandwich while Harry soaked.

Harry thought it a cold thing to do, but that was Darling all over.

The strawberry on a toothpick attached to the sandwich crust was Lolly Paringo all over.

Inspired by the heart-shape of the strawberry, Harry made a stab in the dark. "Tell Lolly you love her. Don't waste your —"

"Out you get," Darling said.

Harry emerged from the bath, blue and dripping.

"No waiver?" he quipped.

"Not unless you want to indemnify yourself against yourself." Darling ate the strawberry, and the faintest of smiles flitted across his face.

"I don't." Harry walked to Rachel's tank and laid his hand

against the panel, touching the eternity ring that waited for who-knew-when. "Love you, Rach. Take good care of our little time traveller, and I'll see you in the morning. One of these mornings."

He climbed into his own tank and strapped on the exoskeleton.

Think of me.

Always and forever.

Doctor Darling touched his wrist. "Okay, Harry. Count backwards from ten."

"Ten, ni —"

The Elydian Dawn series continues with Book 5, Flotsam.

ABOUT THE AUTHOR

Sally Odgers is a Tasmanian wife and mother, grandmother, writer, reader, dog-lover, and tender of labyrinthine websites. She is fascinated by names and loves music and flowers. Sally has been writing fantasy and science fiction for decades and loves creating new realities and series where characters wander in and out of one another's stories. One of her favourites is the Fairy in the Bed series which her alter ego Lark Westerly writes for eXtasy Books. Sally and her husband are co-writers of a number of dog series for children.

To find out more, visit the launching pad of Sally's website world at http://sallybyname.weebly.com or go directly to the Elydian Dawn series home page at https://elydiandawn.weebly.com

Rachel Outward Bound is the fourth book in the series. Books one, two and three are *Elysian Dawn, The Silvering* and *New Dreams*.

www.ingramcontent.com/pod-product-compliance
Lightning Source LLC
Chambersburg PA
CBHW070824120626
46556CB00002B/652